QUEEN'S RANSOM

A FOG CITY NOVEL

LAYLA REYNE

Cover Design: The Book Brander

Cover Photography: Wander Aguiar Photography

Editing: Susie Selva Lori Parks

First Edition

March, 2021

E-Book ISBN: 978-1-7341753-6-3

Paperback ISBN: 978-1-7341753-8-7

ABOUT THIS BOOK

Anywhere close to us is dangerous.

Helena fell in love with Celia from across a hospital bed.
Life has only gotten more deadly since.
And Helena's crush on her sister-in-law more intense.

Celia's putting her life back together after leaving her
abusive ex.
Helena's interest is a welcome boost of confidence.
But the ice queen is more finicky than the engines Celia
rebuilds.

Until Celia and her kids are threatened, and Helena shifts
into overdrive.

Together under one roof, Celia's warmth melts Helena's
heart.
And Celia witnesses the loyalty and love she could have.
Helena may be an assassin, but she makes Celia feel safe.

And brave, which she'll need to rescue the haven she's found.

Queen's Ransom is the fourth book in the Fog City series. This sapphic romantic suspense can be read as a standalone but is best enjoyed after reading books one through three of the series.

For Susie,
who wouldn't let me quit on this one (and who kept me in
Dunkin' until I crossed the finish line).

ONE

The Ducati was running hot—so was Helena—and her favorite mechanic... ice cold. Celia Perri didn't seem to want to help her with either problem. Stretched across the front fender of a mint-condition SS, Celia didn't bother to lift her gaze from the engine she was knuckle-deep in. Cast in the waning light of day, the woman and the car were sexier than they had any right to be.

Forcing down a growl, Helena cut the Duc's engine, kicked the stand into place, and dismounted. She removed her helmet and shook out her hair, using the motion as an excuse to case the shop. Besides the Chevelle, there was only one other vehicle inside the garage—a Bentley jacked up on blocks the next bay over. The coverall-clad legs under the sedan's bumper bent, and Lorenzo, Celia's second at the shop, rolled out from beneath the car.

"Miss Madigan." Smiling, he propped himself on his elbows on the dolly, the patches of gray hair on either side of his chrome dome sticking out Einstein style. "Been a while since we seen you."

Celia's eyes flicked up. Brief but long enough for Helena to glimpse the ice there, same as Helena had cast Celia's way two months ago at the joint birthday party for Celia's daughter and Helena's niece. About what Helena expected —and deserved.

"Work kept me out of town." She stopped outside the bay doors, close enough to speak to Lorenzo while keeping an eye on Celia. "Longer than I wanted to be, but I'm home now." Celia straightened, wiping her hands on a shop rag and continuing to ignore Helena. "Bike sat for too long while I was gone," Helena said, pushing a little harder. "Seems my brothers can't be bothered to treat her right. Could use a tune-up."

The Chevelle's hood slammed shut. "Hey, Zo." Celia finally spoke. "Why don't you go ahead and call it a day."

"I can take a look at the bike for Miss Madigan."

The old man had always been sweet on her, or the bike, Helena wasn't one hundred percent sure. Probably both. But she hadn't come to the shop for his attention. Celia saved her from making an excuse, crossing into Lorenzo's bay and stretching a hand down to him.

"No worries. I've got it." She helped him to his feet and patted his shoulder. "Get an early start on the weekend. We're still waiting on the brakes for the princess anyway."

The chill in her husky voice made Helena think she wasn't only talking about the Bentley. Again, what Helena deserved.

Lorenzo, thankfully, didn't seem to pick up on the undercurrent. "All right, then. Not gonna argue that." He ran his greasy hands down the front of his coveralls and flashed Helena another smile. "Miss Madigan, Cee's the best there is with the bikes. You're in good hands."

"That's why I bring my baby here now." Ever since she'd met the best mechanic in San Francisco.

And the hottest.

When Celia had barreled into her brother, Chris's, hospital room last summer, Helena had lost her breath. For a split second, she'd forgotten all about Chris, the gunshot victim in the bed, and her own missing brother Hawes. She'd been captivated by the gorgeous stranger with long brown hair and blazing brown eyes. Lust at first sight, and fast on its heels, blinding anger at whomever had delivered the black eye and split lip Celia had hastily covered with makeup. Celia's bruises were gone now, along with her abusive ex-husband. The fire in her eyes was out too, at least where Helena was concerned.

The chill radiating off Celia was enough to keep Helena lingering outside the bay doors, waiting as Lorenzo washed up, said goodbye, and climbed into his truck. His taillights had just cleared the yard's gate when the hydraulic lift in the bay closest to the office powered on.

"Bring her over here," Celia called.

Helena walked the bike to the half-sized bay, this one outfitted for motorcycles. Once the single-platform lift was in place, Celia dropped the ramp and Helena rolled the Duc onto the platform. She positioned the front wheel in the padded vise for Celia to clamp in, held the bike steady as Celia attached stability wires on either side of the seat, then stepped out of the way so Celia could raise the lift.

All without saying a word. They didn't need them. They'd performed this routine a dozen times last summer and fall. Helena had had Celia rebuild a perfectly good engine and fix other things on the Duc that didn't need fixing, all so she could spend more time in Celia's presence.

So she could watch in awe as Celia worked with her hands and tools, making an already exceptional machine even better. So she could revel in the heat and wallow in desire whenever Celia bit her bottom lip, the same way Helena would like to—

"You're back," Celia said, cutting short the familiar fantasy.

Helena shifted to relieve the throb between her legs and so she could see Celia on the other side of the lift. "Flew home today."

Celia placed a small drainage bucket under the engine and used a wrench to open gaskets and check fluids, pulling out this dipstick or that. "For how long this time?"

"No plans to leave again anytime soon." It had taken longer than anticipated to cut ties with certain business associates and to shore up connections with others, but she and Hawes were happy with their current slate of contacts and contracts. Jobs that fit the new rules—no indiscriminate killing, no collateral damage, no unvetted targets. Jobs their operatives could handle going forward, allowing Helena breathing room for her attorney job… and maybe also for a life. "I have client meetings and matters at the courthouse," she said. "And the wedding at the end of the month." Their brothers were tying the knot.

"Ah, so that's why you're back."

"In part."

Dark eyes cut to hers—a flash of curiosity—then Celia turned and wove a path into the bowels of the shop. "I'm sure the boys and Lily will be happy to have you back."

Helena circled to the other side of the bike and leaned her hip against a stack of tires. "How are they?"

"You didn't see them first?" Celia asked over the clank and clatter of tool cabinets opening and closing.

"No one was at the house when I got in." Even before she'd left, Hawes had been at the family home less and less, having moved into Chris's renovated condo, and his fraternal twin, Holt, had been spending more and more of his restless nights remodeling the murder house he'd bought in Pacifica. Helena had taken ten minutes to love on the family cats, then gone straight to the shop, to the place and person she'd most wanted to see. "So I came here."

Celia emerged from the shadows of the garage, supplies in hand. She spread them out on a rag at the edge of the platform—filters, washers, belts, spark plugs, and a quart of oil. She turned her back to Helena. "You didn't have to."

Helena waited for Celia to get the first timing belt off, lowered in her right hand, before she made her move. Hooking her toe in the belt's loop, Helena kicked out and pulled Celia off-balance. But only for a second. Shifting into a lunge, Celia yanked the shop rag out from under the parts and chucked it at Helena's face, her fist following in its wake, using her momentum to power the swing.

Helena batted aside the rag and blocked the jab with a raised forearm, catching Celia's weight against her. "Good," she said. "You've been practicing." While Helena had blocked the landing, Celia's quick correction and subsequent action, making use of what she had on hand for self-defense, would buy her time against an unsuspecting attacker. Such as her ex-husband, if that idiot ever showed his face again.

As far as Helena was concerned, all Celia had to do to get the upper hand against her was ask. Fire back in her eyes, a flush streaking across her cheeks, a long brown curl escaping her ponytail, Celia was fucking stunning. And so fucking close after months of personal and physical distance. Close enough to smell the shop grease, the lingering traces of Dove soap, and the strong Italian coffee Celia kept on constant brew at the shop.

Until Celia pushed against Helena's forearm and righted herself, resurrecting the distance between them. "Cruz doesn't exactly take no for an answer."

"Mel's a good teacher." The FBI agent turned bounty hunter was the only person who could best Helena in hand-to-hand combat. She was a certified badass and a friend. One Helena had trusted to protect and train Celia during her absence.

"She is." Celia knelt to pick up the scattered parts. "Dependable."

Unlike her. Direct hit. Helena muffled her sharp inhale and knelt beside Celia. "Fuck, Cee. I'm sorry."

Celia whipped her face the opposite direction and the avoidance fucking stung. Deserved, but stung. Helena picked up the last spark plug and placed it with the others in Celia's rag. "I'm sorry," she said again.

Celia stood and laid the rag full of parts on the platform, neatly spreading them out again. "You didn't promise me anything."

"I promised to be your friend." Helena rose but didn't step back. "To help you." She'd wanted to promise more, offer more, but between wanting to give Celia space to work through her divorce and juggling her own obligations —succeeding Hawes as assassin-in-chief and managing a grueling year-end wrongful convictions caseload—she'd done the opposite of promising or offering more. She'd overcommitted, pulled back, then fled. And now so had Celia.

"You sent Mel," Celia said as she removed and replaced spark plugs. "And I knew Chris and your brothers had my back."

"It's not the same." The next time Celia's face was angled her direction, Helena grasped her chin. Not to force her gaze, but to get a closer look, to run her thumb across Celia's smooth skin and see if there was any discoloration beneath the layer of foundation.

Nothing, thank fuck.

"Have you heard from him?" Helena asked.

"Not a peep." Celia shook her head, dislodging Helena's hold. "Do I have the Madigans to thank for that?"

Celia didn't know the full scope of their operations, but she wasn't blind. She'd been there for Chris during his and Hawes's shit last summer, during their grandmother's attempted coup. She knew the Madigans did more than run a cold storage business, and Chris's past career as an ATF agent—before he'd become an in-house investigator for the Madigans—had taught Celia to not ask questions she didn't want the answers to. Her discretion and her acceptance of their atypical reality were two of the many reasons Helena liked her so much.

"That," Helena conceded, "plus a restraining order and an airtight divorce judgment."

Celia finished replacing the second timing belt. "You don't know Dex like I do. He always comes back."

Helena grasped the timing belt and gave it a gentle tug, drawing Celia's attention. "If he does, he's gonna find things have changed. You're not alone, Cee. You never will be again."

Appreciation and relief eased the tightness around Celia's mouth and eyes, softening her features. A crack in the glacier. Helena would take that, valued it more than any desire she'd hoped for. Celia deserved comfort and peace after too long without it. She wasn't much older than Helena, and she'd already raised two kids into their teens and taken over her late father's garage, all while dealing with a worthless ex who cheated, abused, and frequently disappeared.

Like Helena had. She didn't want to make that mistake again. "I'm sorry, Cee. Truly."

A blink, a nod, and another flash of heat in Celia's dark eyes. That morphed into anger as tires squealed on the road outside the yard fence, the accompanying growl of an engine growing louder. "Assholes." Celia tossed the timing belt aside and stepped toward the bay door. "They act like the road out there is a drag strip, never mind the parks at either end of the street."

Except run-of-the-mill assholes who pretended to be speed demons usually drove BMWs, preferred the left or center lane, and forgot to cut their lights as they sped up.

The black Charger that slashed across lanes of traffic *toward* the curb in front of the shop, just on the other side of the chain-link fence around the yard, gaining speed with its lights off in the dusky twilight, did not appear to be driven by the average run-of-the-mill asshole.

Celia registered the same reality, her eyes going wide. "What the—"

Helena grabbed her by the wrist and yanked her back inside the bay. "Get down!" Spinning them, she curled over and around Celia, moving them into a crouch behind the stack of tires. She blindly flailed out an arm, searching for anything that could work as a weapon. Her fingers closed around a wrench as a hail of bullets pinged the exterior metal walls of the garage. Glass shattered a bay over, and beneath her, Celia screamed.

"Stay down!" Hand to Celia's back, making sure she stayed low and out of sight, Helena peeked over the top of the tire stack. Was it a drive-by or an incoming attack? Neither, it seemed, as the Charger screeched to a halt outside the opening in the yard gate. If she'd been alone, Helena might have taken advantage of the narrow window of surprise and gone on offense. But she wasn't alone. She had to play defense. "How do I get the garage doors down?" That had never been something she'd needed to look for before.

"Red button," Celia replied, voice shaky but clear. "Between the bay doors. Double tap for the gate too."

Helena calculated her steps and the evasive maneuvers she needed to make to cross the several exposed feet to her target. Not quick enough. Another flurry of gunfire erupted. Not aimed directly at or into the garage bays but at the offices and customer waiting area. More glass shattered.

Damage, then. That's what they were after.

The fast and furious second assault ended, and the Charger's driver revved the V8. Tires smoking, it shot off down the street, bouncing like a pinball between cars to a cacophony of answering horns.

Escaping.

Helena shoved the wrench into Celia's hand. "Stay down!"

Spinning, she grabbed two throwing knives out of the Duc's saddle bag and ran flat out toward the opening in the gate. She reached the sidewalk in time to see the Charger's dented fender disappear around the corner. Too late to throw a knife at its tires, much less get a read on the plates, and too late to give chase, judging by the roaring engine and second wave of car horns a street over.

Not that Helena would risk leaving Celia exposed in the shop, unprotected if the Charger made a second pass. Chris would never forgive her. And she'd never forgive herself.

"Fuck!"

Holding both knives in one hand, she dug out her phone with the other and sent an SOS to Holt, trusting he'd distribute the call for help accordingly. As soon as Helena stepped back into the yard, the chain-link fence began to roll closed behind her, Celia operating it from inside. And as soon as she stepped inside the garage bay, Celia banged the red button a second time, the wrench still clenched in her fist.

"What the hell was that?" Her voice shook with the same tremors that visibly rippled through her body, but her dark eyes blazed. She was both terrified and furious.

"A message," Helena replied.

"For who?"

"*That's* the million-dollar question." And Helena didn't like any of the potential answers.

TWO

Three hours later, Celia's head was still spinning. The fact she was climbing the steps of the Madigan family home with her mom and kids in tow only made it spin faster.

Celia had visited the Pac Heights mansion several times before to train with Helena, her daughter Mia more often as a babysitter for Holt's toddler, and Chris most often as Hawes's fiancé, but it was the first visit for Marco and Gloria and the first time they'd all been there together.

Mia led the procession, a box of pastries in hand. Beside Celia, her mother, Gloria, *ooh*ed and *aah*ed at the Victorian's extensive restorations. Marco, walking behind them with Chris, was too busy being a punk, as thirteen-year-old boys were prone to do.

"Uncle Dante," he said, using the nickname bestowed on Chris by his late ATF partner. "You snagged a sugar daddy."

Chris thumped the back of his head and chided in kind. "Watch it, Plato."

"Blame it on the hunger trolls in my belly." He patted

his stomach and side-eyed Celia. "We are *way* past dinner time."

Another problem with thirteen-year-old boys; they'd eat you out of house and home, the latter of which Celia had uprooted them from at Helena's insistence. Chris, who'd met them at the garage—*the crime scene*—had backed the play, leaving Celia little choice but to go along with them, not that she disagreed with the logic of it. Celia shivered. She didn't know all the particulars of what the Madigans were into, but she knew it was more than cold storage, and she knew they fiercely protected their own. She'd graciously accept that protection to keep her mom and kids safe. Celia never wanted them to experience the terror she had felt earlier, hiding for her safety, scared for her life and legacy, afraid for the life and safety of the woman with her.

The woman who'd beaten them there, judging by the Ducati in the driveway next to where they'd parked. But it was Hawes, dressed in a suit despite the evening hour, who opened the front door. "I think I can help with the food problem," he said, clearly having overheard Marco's protest.

Warm air rushed from inside, and on it wafted aromas of fire-baked dough, rich spicy marinara, and melted cheese.

Marco's eyes widened, round as saucers. "Is that Tony's?"

Hawes stepped out of the doorway and invited them in with a sweep of his arm. "Only the best pizza in town for family weekend."

"Yes!" Marco dropped his bags in the foyer and followed his nose to the dining room where pizza boxes were spread the length of the long table. He pumped his fist. "Family weekend was the best idea ever."

"Told ya," Chris said with a wink. Credit to her brother and his undercover skills for coming up with the idea. A blending of the families culminating in the wedding cake tasting at their cousin Angelica's bakery on Sunday. It was as good a cover story as any for why they were spending the weekend at the Madigans' instead of at home.

Celia pushed Marco's bags out of the middle of the foyer, then set hers and Gloria's atop them against the stairwell wall. "I swear he has manners."

"He did," Mia said, adding her bulging duffel to the stack. "And then they magically vanished with puberty. *Poof*!"

"Hey!" Marco protested around a bite of pizza.

She rolled her eyes and offered the pink box of pastries to Hawes. "Accept these as our apology."

Beside him, Chris peeked into the box. "I'm claiming the mistletoe cannoli." It was weeks past season but there were perks to being family and perks to Mia also working at AB's.

"Apparently," Celia said, shooting judging glares at both her brother and son, "the lack of manners is contagious."

"Yeah!" Marco said. "It's Uncle Dante's fault."

"Judgment free zone," Hawes said with a bemused smirk.

Celia chuckled. "Let's see how you feel by Sunday."

"He's stuck with us now." Gloria rose on her toes and kissed her future son-in-law's cheek. "Thank you for having us." She'd been a fan of Hawes since their first meeting. The Madigan patriarch turned on the charm any time she was around, belying the lingering chill about him Celia could never quite put her finger on. Even if Hawes were outwardly chilly to them, Celia didn't think Gloria would care. Hawes had given Chris a reason to come home and stay home; that's all that mattered to Gloria. And to Celia. Their family whole again after ten long years—and it was expanding.

"We're happy to have you," Hawes said. "Go eat." He gestured at the bags. "We'll get all this sorted after."

Gloria and Mia followed Marco into the dining room, and Celia was glad the ruse had worked. Her family was safe and on the way to being satisfied, at least where their bellies were concerned.

"Is Brax with you?"

She turned to find the biggest Madigan had emerged from the living room with the tiniest one—his daughter, Lily—in his inked right arm. The dichotomy between Holt and Hawes always gave Celia a second's pause. While Hawes shared many physical traits with Helena—cool blue eyes, pale skin, lighter hair, and sharp features—his fraternal twin was all bulk and muscle, freckled skin, tattoos, warm brown eyes, and a mess of wavy hair that was closer to auburn than blond, especially in the winter. Ditto his full beard. And it wasn't only the physical differences between the brothers. There was no sense of cold about Holt Madigan. For all his bulk, he reminded Celia of the flannel-dressed stuffed bear Mia had once created at a Build-A-Bear party.

Those usual differences, however, were not what made her almost gasp. With pronounced bags under his bloodshot eyes, his skin an unhealthy pale, and his Raptors tee and jeans days old and wrinkled, Holt looked more like one of those sad teddy bears from movies or internet memes than he did the cheery one Mia had brought home.

"He went back to the station," Chris answered.

Holt's misery visibly worsened, then plummeted further as Lily spit out her pacifier and demanded "Ba-Ba!"

Celia's first instinct was to glance around for a blanket or bottle, but then the pain that ghosted across Holt's face, together with the earlier mention of Chief Kane, made it clear who both father and daughter were missing.

Before any of them breached the awkward abyss, Mia rejoined them, oblivious to the tension. "There's my birthday twin." She ruffled Lily's auburn curls. "I've missed you."

"Sorry about that," Holt mumbled. "We've been at—" He caught himself, like he wasn't supposed to say something, then corrected. "Out at the coast. Project there."

"Can I hold her?"

"Mia," Celia lightly chided. Her daughter loved spending time with Lily, and Celia loved that for her, but she also sensed the toddler was one of the few things holding her father together right then.

Holt, though, smiled, his inner warmth cracking through the outer misery. "She'd like that." He shifted Lily into Mia's arms, and Mia cradled her close as she wandered back to the dining room. At a loss for what to do with his hands, Holt raked one through his hair and skirted the other over his beard, making a bigger mess of both. Only Helena appearing from the living room with his tablet seemed to give him purpose again. "Footage downloaded?" he asked.

She nodded, handed him the tablet, and cut a glance through all of them in the foyer. "We need to talk."

The happy family veneer dissolved and the real reason they were there zoomed again to the forefront of Celia's mind.

"Go on," Gloria said from the end of the dining table. She knelt, a small piece of cheese in each hand, to lure the cats circling Helena's ankles into the dining room. "Come here, girls." Once Daisy and Tulip were in her thrall, enticed by their favorite food, Gloria stood and wiped her hands on her jeans. "I'll hold the fort here." She knew something was up, but she wouldn't pry. She'd had to learn that lesson with an ATF agent for a son.

Celia had had to learn the same lesson, which was another reason why tonight was so head spinning. She was on the inside for a change, and she didn't like it one bit. She and the family business had been directly threatened. Her mom and her kids could be next. She eyed the mansion's street-facing windows. "Are they safe down here?"

"Yes," Holt said, a certainty in his voice that had been lacking a minute ago. He tapped the tablet screen a few quick times, then handed it to Celia. Displayed onscreen were a dozen different views of the house—interior and exterior—including the street out front and the corners at either end of the block. "We'll know if any danger is coming."

She handed the tablet back. "Thank you."

"We can talk in there"—Helena jutted a thumb at the living room—"or upstairs."

"Upstairs," Celia said with a glance toward the dining room. "I don't want to chance them overhearing." While she was okay knowing certain aspects of the Madigans' business, she wasn't okay involving the rest of her family.

Instinct—and Chris's life the past six months—cautioned against it. "If that's okay with you all?"

Chris and the gathered Madigans nodded.

Helena smirked. "Your chance to peek behind the curtain."

Celia didn't mention that *The Wizard of Oz* was one of her least favorite movies of all time. Instead, she popped into the dining room, kissed the tops of her kids' heads and her mother's cheek, then followed the others upstairs, steeling herself for whatever she was about to see or hear. As with Chris's job before, and with Helena's and the Madigans' now, she tended to test the limits of how much she could or should know. She'd pushed too hard in the past, pushed her brother too far. She didn't want to risk that distance again, didn't want to put any more strain on their reunited and growing family, but she also had to trust the Madigans and Chris to decide how much she needed to know.

No amount of trust or mental coaching, however, could have prepared her for what she saw when she crested the stairs into the bonus room at the top of the Madigan family home. Helena had often referred to the room as "the lair," but Celia had written that off as hyperbole or a teasing joke. Setting foot in the room for the first time, Celia quickly decided *lair* was a massive understatement. One half of the space was what you'd expect of a bonus room often inhabited by a toddler. A crib and mobile were tucked in the window alcove, a rocking chair sat where a desk chair should in the corner of an L-shaped desk, and toys were scattered on the floor around a seating area comprised of a plush couch and two high-backed chairs. And then there was the other half of the room. The entire right wall looked like one of those massive computer setups in a blockbuster action movie. An industrial desk ran the length of the wall, keyboards resting on its ledge. Beneath it were multiple computer units, and above it, almost to the ceiling, stretched a wall of monitors and speakers.

Holt skirted around her and claimed one of the two rolling chairs in front of his... command center. Was that the right word? A flurry of keystrokes later and several of the screens went dark before Celia could even comprehend what she'd seen on them. Good. She didn't need that much of a peek. A small yet firm hand landed on her lower back, and Helena directed her to the seating area, sinking onto the sofa beside her. Not touching, but close enough for comfort and reassurance. Celia wasn't too proud to admit she needed both after the day's chaos.

Hawes perched on the arm of the high-backed chair across from them, angled toward Holt. "What do we know?"

Several other monitors flickered on. "That's the street outside the shop," Celia said, recognizing and comprehending the images this time.

Holt nodded. "Surveillance from the shop cameras and from traffic cams and ATMs."

He rewound the footage to the moment Celia's world had started to spin. Not in the good way, not like the first time she'd laid eyes on Helena Madigan. One look at the petite blond at Chris's hospital bedside and hummingbirds had taken flight in Celia's belly, making her lightheaded and making her forget, for a few precious seconds, all the bad things that had happened to her that awful week. *This* was not *that* feeling. Onscreen, a black Charger, its lights off, veered around the corner two blocks away from the shop. It swerved across lanes of traffic, pulled alongside the shop's gate, and opened fire, bullets and sparks pinging off the shop's metal walls. All the bad things that had happened during the awful day were drawn into sharp, deadly focus.

"That's the car," Helena said.

And sharper still as Holt paused the playback and zoomed in on the car's rear bumper as it turned the corner at the other end of the street. "We've got a partial on the plate," Holt said. "Arizona. I'll get it processing."

"The bullets?" Hawes asked.

Chris gathered his long dark hair into a messy top knot and spun the desk chair next to Holt so he could straddle it backward. "SFPD is processing. We're being kept in the loop."

"Tire tracks?"

"Not enough to do us any good, but we don't need it. We've got enough to work with from the cameras."

The rapid-fire back-and-forth among the Madigans and Chris continued, making Celia's world spin faster. As did another paused image onscreen. A gun perched on the shadowed passenger window frame, aimed directly at the shop.

Celia's mind transported her back there and she relived those terrifying few minutes. Helena grabbing her by the wrist and yanking her down. Helena curling her body over hers, muffling each of Celia's shouts and jerks as bullets pinged off metal, louder and worse than any hailstorm Celia had ever experienced. The crack of glass. A brief silence, then another round of gunfire. The absolute terror when the gunfire ceased, and Helena left her. Celia hadn't feared for her own safety but for Helena's.

A thigh brushed against hers, and Helena curled an arm

around her shoulders. "Breathe, Cee," she said. "Just breathe."

"Someone shot up the shop."

"Shock," Hawes said. "Blanket?"

Holt moved about the room, but Celia's mind barely acknowledged it, still caught several hours before back in the garage. "The busted window in the Bentley, in the office, in the waiting area… Shit, I didn't look to see if the SS was hit."

"I'm sure it's fine." Helena squeezed her shoulder. "I didn't notice any damage to it."

Holt handed a blanket to Helena, who folded it around Celia's shoulders. The baby powder scent calmed the spinning a little. "That's Whiskey Walker's SS."

"He's a friend," Holt said. "It'll be okay."

"And he's used to being shot at," Chris added.

Celia pulled the blanket around her tighter, grateful Helena's arm came with it. "Who would shoot up the shop?"

"That's what we're going to find out," Helena said.

Chris rolled across the floor, close enough to lay a hand on Celia's forearm. "We're going to sort this out. We just have to consider all the possibilities."

"Were you having trouble with anyone at the shop?" Hawes asked. "Employees or customers? Anyone from Arizona?"

She shook her head. "We're a small, tight-knit crew. No issues there, and none with customers. And we've had no Arizona customers that I can recall. Like I told Chief Kane, we're just a local shop."

"That services high-end autos."

"Why would anyone shoot those up?"

"One of those cars was Jameson Walker's." Helena's gaze skipped to her brothers. "Message to his crew?"

"Why?" Celia said. "He's a basketball coach?"

"Who's famous," Hawes said. "And married to the agent in charge of the FBI's San Francisco field office."

"Whose family is stupid rich," Holt added, "and has old school IRA enemies."

The IRA shot up the shop? Wait… "Like that boat thing a few years back?"

"It's a possibility," Chris said. "But I think it's unlikely."

"Who'd the Bentley belong to?" Helena asked.

"Bill Patrick. He just sold his ranch in Paso Robles. The Bentley was a retirement present to himself. First car he's ever owned that wasn't a truck."

"What about your ex?" Hawes said.

Now there was a possibility more likely than the IRA, except… "I haven't seen Dex since last year, and why would he shoot up the shop? If he's not gonna pay child support, I have to have the means to take care of our kids."

"Let me rephrase," Hawes said. "Does Dex have trouble with anyone?"

A bitter laugh escaped her lips. Of course, Dex strikes again. Not in person, but no less damaging.

"We're gonna need names," Chris said.

"You know that internet meme with the guy who unfurls a scroll-length list?" Cringes greeted her all around; yeah, they all knew which one. "That's what we're talking about here and that's just the people I know about."

"Write them down," Helena said with another gentle squeeze of her shoulders. "The sooner we figure out who did this, the sooner you can get back to fixing the princess."

So Helena had caught her earlier choice of words. Celia,

though, was stuck on the first part of Helena's sentence. "Why can't the police figure this out?"

"They can," Hawes said. "But we may be able to do it faster."

And make it go away? Like they had Dex?

"Until then," Helena said, "get comfy. We've got plenty of food and plenty of room."

"Are you sure?" She directed her question at Hawes and Holt. "Chris and Helena came up with this plan at the scene. We didn't get a chance to ask you."

Holt's tired face cracked, a genuine smile peeking out. "Not gonna say no to an army of babysitters."

Hawes slid off the arm of the chair and knelt in front of her, a hand on her knee. "We're family, Celia, and we take care of family."

THREE

There was zero chance Celia could hear them from the main floor, but Helena waited for Holt, who was monitoring her progress onscreen, to confirm she'd reached the dining room. Given the all clear, Helena turned to her brothers and to the unpleasant truth none of them had spoken in Celia's presence. "So, who wants to address the elephant in the room?"

Hawes didn't hesitate; it wasn't his way. "*We* might have been the target of that drive-by."

A grim reality that had taken root in Helena's mind as soon as she'd secured Celia's safety. *This* was exactly why she'd pulled away from Celia last fall, why she'd stayed away while conducting her negotiations, and why she knew better than to go to the shop today. And yet she'd still gone, unable to resist. She'd missed the spark of attraction, the banter, the friendship, the hours spent with someone outside their world. And after months neck deep in it, she'd needed that. Desperately. But had she risked Celia's life to get it?

"Did you pick up any tails on the way over there?" Hawes asked.

"None that I noticed."

"Why were you at the shop anyway?" Chris said. "I tuned up the Duc last week."

Kicking out a foot, she shoved the base of Chris's chair, for the sass and to make room to skirt by and flop onto the couch. "Your sister is a better mechanic."

He scoffed in mock outrage.

Hawes shoved him from the other side. "She's right." He moved off the arm of the chair and into the seat, crossing one leg over the other and painting on his pondering face. "You're sure all the meetings went well?" he asked Helena.

She slumped into the couch cushions, tapping each of her fingernails against her thumbnail—right hand, left hand, repeat. She'd strived to break the nervous habit but wasn't always successful. She didn't hide it from her family. They all had their ticks: Hawes pacing circles, Holt typing frenetically, Chris muttering to his dead partner, Brax running a hand over his head. "As far as I knew," she said, "we were square with most everyone. Negotiations took time, but there were no objections to our realignment. Some grumbling from those who have to solicit new contracts, but for the others like us, it helps their businesses." With the Madigans more selective of their targets, there were more contracts on the table for the less selective.

"Regardless, we need to make our own list," Hawes said.

"Start with Rose's contacts," Chris suggested.

Except those were the first meetings on Helena's road-show. "We've settled those accounts. They backed the wrong horse. They know it." She scooted over, tucking a leg under herself and making room for Holt, who'd abandoned his command center to join them. "And again, we're helping their bottom line, not hurting it."

"You *think*," Chris said.

"You think this could be Rose?" Holt asked.

Helena suspected his rumbled question would have been a growl if her brother weren't so damn exhausted. As the months had passed, Holt's every mention of their incarcerated grandmother grew more hostile. There was a storm brewing there, and God help them all when it finally blew ashore.

"We can't discount the possibility," Hawes replied.

"Behind Rose," Helena said, acknowledging the possibility but wanting to move on from it before Holt exploded, "the most likely parties would be those who are adversely affected by our shift in objectives."

"Those most likely to be your targets," Chris said.

Helena smirked. "Bonus points for Mr. Hair."

"You get on those lists," Hawes said to her. "And include anyone your meetings didn't go well with. You said *most* earlier. I want to know about the outliers. Full debrief tomorrow."

She nodded and crossed her legs. "I'll loop in Avery," she said, referring to their top lieutenant who had served as her second at all the meetings. "She may have noticed something I didn't."

"Good," Hawes said, then angled toward his fiancé. "Now, tell us about Dex."

Like Hawes earlier, Chris didn't hesitate, his low *low* opinion of his ex-brother-in-law on the tip of his tongue. "He's an abusive, neglectful, self-centered asshole."

Helena flitted a hand. "Old news." She was more inter-ested in where she suspected Hawes's train of thought had been going. "Was Dex tangled up with someone who might do this?"

"You asked Celia—"

"And *you're* the trained investigator. I don't believe for a second you didn't dig into him and what he'd been up to during your absence."

He narrowed his dark eyes. "You're annoyingly perceptive."

"Which is why she's now in charge of this whole shebang," Hawes said, flitting his hand in a similar fashion. "Answer her question."

Chris slid his narrow-eyed glare to the side. "Traitor." Helena had to stifle a laugh, but the tiny bubble of hilarity popped with Chris's next words. "Celia doesn't know the half of it." He leaned forward, elbows on his knees. "Dex was always into this scheme or that. Fucker can drive. That's what brought him around the shop in the first place, and that's what made him the getaway driver of choice for certain low-level criminal elements. Celia thinks it's all loan-shark kinds of shit, of which there's plenty, but that wasn't all of it. Dex was the king of bad decisions. I half suspect that's why he ran off so often. To lie low."

"*That*," Helena said, "and he couldn't keep his dick in his pants."

"That too," Chris conceded. "I'll supplement Celia's list."

"Why didn't any of this come up during the divorce?" Hawes asked.

"We didn't need it." Helena uncrossed her legs, folded one back under herself, and braced an elbow on the inside of her knee. She held up a hand to count off on her fingers. "One, he didn't contest the divorce. Two, we had pictures and witness statements to prove physical and emotional abuse. Three, we had evidence of the adultery too."

"What about the garage?" Hawes asked. "Does he have any stake in it?"

"Fuck no," Chris spat. "The business part of it is incorporated, and the property sits on land held in a family trust. Dad set all that up."

"And Celia did nothing to commute it," Helena further explained. "All accounts are separate. We did the full accounting for the divorce."

"Doesn't exclude the shop as a target," Hawes said.

Helena agreed, even if Dex didn't have a stake in Perri Auto Works. She mentally kicked herself for not doing more to secure the place and keep Celia safe. Yes, she'd been training Celia in self-defense, but more was needed. "Security?" she asked Chris.

"Some but nothing like the package here or at MCS headquarters."

"I'll rectify that," Holt said.

Her brother's sudden reentry into the conversation startled Helena. Holt had always been the quietest of them, but quiet was too generous a description for him lately. Even when she hadn't been there in person, she had sensed his withdrawal over calls and video. It worried Helena, reminded her of his withdrawal after their parents' death when no one had been able to reach him. No one except Braxton Kane. Fourteen years ago, Brax had snapped Holt out of his malaise, and until last fall, Brax hadn't gone a week without talking to or seeing his best friend, despite the conflicts of interest inherent in a friendship between the chief of police and a digital assassin. After Lily was born, Brax had barely gone a few days without a visit, the top cop adorably enamored with his goddaughter. The fact he'd become a ghost the past few months made zero sense, and Helena didn't buy his work excuse for a minute. End of year was always busy for SFPD; this one no different than the last. Something else was going on with Brax.

"So, we make our lists too," Hawes said, snapping her back to the present problem. "Work them all."

Everyone nodded, the meeting effectively adjourned. Even if there had been more to say, Lily put a final stop to it, her cry transmitted over the one-way baby monitor connected to Holt's setup.

He bolted to his feet, parental instinct on high alert, especially with Lily teething lately. "That's my cue."

"I'll head down too." Chris stood and patted his belly. "There better be some pizza and pastries left."

"I'll join you," Hawes said and accepted Chris's offered hand.

Helena rose and crossed in front of them. She'd stashed some legal pads in the corner desk. "I'll get started on my lists."

Hawes grasped her wrist, stopping her midstride. "No."

She reined in her defensive instincts and arched a brow instead. "No?"

"You were almost shot today."

"Not the first time."

Hawes's gaze flicked to the couch and back. "You spent the last twenty minutes fidgeting on that couch."

"The past three hours," Chris said. "But who's counting?"

She wrenched her wrist free so she could flip off her annoying future brother.

Chuckling, Hawes gently covered her hand. "You need to blow off some steam, Hena."

"So does my sister," Chris added. "She's not obvious about it, but she rarely is. Everyone else comes first for her."

Helena smirked. "What are you suggesting, Mr. Hair? House is a bit crowded for—"

Chris blushed and sputtered. "Sparring! Training!"

His mortification was all the revenge Helena needed, but she played it up some more for fun, jutting out her lip in mock disappointment. In reality, no matter how much she wanted to do more than spar with Celia, she shouldn't make another move until Celia was safe, including from her.

Embarrassment tempered, Chris clasped her shoulder. "Make sure my sister can defend herself," he said sincerely. "In case Dex or any of his friends get closer next time."

At least Chris wasn't laying the blame at their feet. Whether for his own sake or theirs, Helena would take the offered out and the offered chance to help. "I can do that."

FOUR

Kids fed and settled into the living room with Gloria, Chris, Hawes, the box of pastries and a movie, Celia followed Helena downstairs to the basement. Much like her mother on first arrival, Celia found something new to admire about the old house with each visit. The intricately carved and restored crenellations and crown moldings, how the tall narrow structure seemed to endlessly sprawl inside, the way all that space somehow managed to feel warm and homey despite its elegance, the blond who moved gracefully through its halls like the family cats.

Celia diverted her attention from the sway of Helena's hips in skin-tight yoga pants. "For future reference, if you ever want to distract my brother, cannoli are key."

Chuckling, Helena led them around the corner and into the state-of-the-art home gym, flipping on the overheads as they entered. "He did seem laser focused on that pastry box."

"He always wants first dibs. Our cousin, Angelica, can

get him to do practically anything with the promise of cannoli."

"Anything?"

Celia pitched her hoodie into the corner. "She's still driving the vintage Mustang he rebuilt for her."

"So cake tasting Sunday is going to be off the hook?"

Celia grinned. "You have no idea."

Helena returned her smile, and the hummingbirds took flight in Celia's stomach again. She rotated away before her thoughts ran off with her actions, distracting herself by taking in the home gym. Not much had changed about the room since she'd last trained there. One half of the room was filled with fitness machines and training stations: a magnetic wall strip with knives and stars behind a throwing lane that dead-ended in a cork strip on the wall; a rowing machine and spin bike; and a bolted-down cage that included TRX bands, a bench press, and free weights. Mats occupied the other half of the space and a mini fridge was tucked in the far corner. Sitting atop the fridge was a stack of folded towels and a basket of combat gear: gloves, garrotes, telescopic sticks, and more. The scent of chlorine lingered, floating in from the infinity pool in the smaller room next door. Neither the gym nor the pool were the original intended use of the house's basement—a food cellar, then an earthquake shelter, then a war bunker, if Celia remembered her local history correctly. The upgrades made it so the Madigans had anything and everything they needed to work out at home. Important on nights when family drama was top of mind, and there seemed to be a lot of those nights. And now it was *Celia's* family drama, on top of whatever other Madigan drama she probably didn't know—or want to know—about.

"We don't have to do this tonight," she said. "You've done enough—"

"Hawes didn't give me a choice." Helena withdrew two water bottles from the fridge and set them on the floor next to the mats. "He ordered me out of the lair. I'm too keyed up, and I imagine you are too."

She wasn't wrong, but if Helena didn't want to be there… "But you don't have to—"

"I'm right where I want to be," she replied, voice gentler, as she lowered herself onto the mat. "I meant what I said at the shop. I owe you better… as a friend." Before Celia could reply, Helena stretched her torso over one leg, hands clasping her foot.

Celia curled her fingers, fighting the desire to reach out and push aside the curtain of gold that hid Helena's face. In part to see her expression, in part to feel if the long blond strands were as soft as they looked. It was a fascinating, attractive dichotomy. Something that appeared so soft, so ethereal, on someone who was otherwise so sharp in her features, words, and focus. Celia wanted to understand the contrast, wanted to understand Helena better, but there were reasons not to reach out. Helena's prior disappearing act, the fact Celia was newly single, the limits around what she could and should know about the Madigans.

But there were also numerous reasons to act. Helena had played a key role in keeping Chris safe and in keeping their family safe last summer, hustling Celia, their mom, and the kids out of town to a safe house when things got dicey. She'd played a bigger role in getting Dex out of her life. Celia didn't think her ex would stay gone—he never did—but for the first time since high school, Celia had space and freedom in her world. She'd thought maybe Helena would like to fill some of that space, help her exercise some of that freedom. Celia was interested, but then Helena had pushed her away, then disappeared altogether.

Stretching the opposite direction, Celia contemplated the vast differences in her life between last January and this one. The fact she was even contemplating acting on her interest in someone the same gender, in someone besides Dex, the only person she'd ever been with, was nearly mind blowing. The attraction part wasn't new. On the rare occasions she'd let herself consider a life after Dex, Celia hadn't limited herself to one gender. Not when she'd seen her brother experience attraction to men and women and not when she herself had felt attraction to all different kinds of people. But acting on it... She'd never had the chance, and now that she did, she was nervous. She felt a bit like a fraud. Could she really call herself pansexual—that was the term she felt best described her sexuality—when she'd only ever been with Dex?

Did she have any business worrying about her sex life at all? Yes, she was single for the first time in a decade and a half, but she had been shot at tonight and had two teen kids, a senior parent, and a business to worry over. She needed to focus on taking care of those things first, and working out and sparring with Helena helped make her better able to do that. To protect the people and things she loved and cared about most. She just had to ignore the attraction that fluttered in her belly whenever Helena was in the same room. Focus instead on being a good friend.

"You know," she said, "the friend thing cuts both ways. You've had a lot of family stuff to sort lately too."

Helena tossed back her hair and switched legs. "So have you."

"And you know about most of mine."

Helena's stretch collapsed, her chest falling onto her knee, and her hair fell forward again. "Cee, I can't…"

Celia acted before she could second-guess herself, using her index finger to draw back the curtain of blond on one side. "My brother was a fed, and now he works for your family. I get there are things you can and can't tell me."

A flicker of a smile. "Always did like that about you."

"But I mean it. The friend thing goes both ways." She withdrew her hand and levered up, waiting for Helena to do the same. "If you need someone to talk to—on a nonincriminating meta level—or just someone to spar with, I can be there for you too."

Helena's smile widened. "Especially while trapped in my house."

Celia laughed. "And after."

Helena pulled her hair into a ponytail, then pulled herself to her feet. "For now," she said, offering Celia a hand up, "let's just work out the ohmigod-we-were-shot-at-tonight stress."

"I feel like that's my internal monologue. Not so much yours."

Helena shrugged. "Closer than you might think."

Celia doubted it, but Helena didn't give her time to dwell, assuming her usual position on the mat. As they circled each other, Helena moved like she was out for a weekend stroll, her limbs loose and posture confident, but her eyes were sharp, tracking Celia's steps. Celia tried to mirror her, tried not to telegraph her maneuvers, but it was hard not to revert to the defensive position she'd spent much of her adult life in.

Helena kicked out first. Celia blocked the kick. A bevy of

jabs and hooks followed, and Celia blocked and dodged, spinning and using her momentum to return a jab. Helena blocked. Celia countered with a kick. Another flurry of motion—hits, kicks, blocks—all while circling. Nothing landed, but the rapid-fire exchange and constant movement had Celia breathing heavy, starting to sweat, and smiling more than she had all day.

Helena was likewise grinning though not the least bit winded. "So, about that Bentley..." Her smile morphed into a crooked, tempting smirk. "When does she get her new brakes?"

"Monday," Celia replied with a smirk of her own. If Helena wanted to word play some more, Celia was down. "She'll still go plenty fast, though."

Celia considered her next attack, then unleashed a sequence of swings and kicks that Mel had taught her. The new moves allowed her to skirt Helena's shoulder with her knuckles, Helena's side with her toes. More than she'd ever landed before. The victory, however, was short lived. Lightning fast, Helena grabbed her by the ankle and took her to the floor. Closing her eyes, Celia caught her breath and smiled as the good kind of adrenaline lit her up from the inside. Fuck, this felt good.

A shadow fell over her. "You're good, yeah?" Helena asked.

Celia opened her eyes and counted the tendrils of blond hanging her direction. Lots of little victories. "Yeah." She clasped Helena's offered hand and bounded back up. "Gotta try that move."

"Good," Helena said. "And good attack, but no brakes next time. Don't hesitate. Don't give me or someone else that extra second to adjust. Just go."

They began to circle again, trading jabs and blocks, as Celia shared a little of herself with her friend. "Been trying to put the brakes on Mia and Ethan, but that's a different story." A relatively normal and mundane topic of conversation. No less worrisome, though. "Only the promise of unlimited Lily time got her on board with the weekend at Casa Madigan plan."

"Ah, young love."

"Young love resulted in me having her, my first kid, at her age and spending half my life in an abusive relationship."

Helena halted on a dime, her fingers twitching at her sides and her icy blue eyes cutting to the knife strip. "If he steps out of line…"

Celia spun, distracting Helena from her murderous intent. She hadn't meant to put Ethan in her sights. "None of the warning signs are there. I'm just being hyper vigilant. Dex was always on his best behavior around Mom. Fooled all of us."

Helena swept her leg low, and Celia hopped over it. "Despite Dex, you raised two great kids."

"I know." She was proud of Mia and Marco and of the job she'd done raising them, effectively as a single parent. She'd kept them out of Dex's line of fire and had strived to give them everything they needed to succeed, day by day and in whatever future they chose. She'd made mistakes, but she'd done her best to keep her kids shielded from them. "I just want better for them."

She and Helena traded upper cuts, jukes, and high knees in another speed round, retreating to their corners after an intense two minutes. "I get that," Helena said. "It's why we made certain changes last year. For Lily and others of her generation to come."

They met again in the center of the mat, and this time Celia didn't hesitate. She sliced a jab across her body, aiming for Helena's opposite shoulder. The hit landed —*triumph*—but then Helena's other arm came up between Celia's still extended arm and her chest—*caught*.

Helena hauled her in close. "That's what took me away the past couple months." Her hold remained firm, but her voice and expression softened. "We're trying to make things better. I'm sorry if I hurt you doing so. That was never my intent."

"You don't have to apologize, but thank you."

Neither moved to break the hold, and this close, Celia could see the beads of sweat glistening at Helena's hairline, could smell her lavender-scented shampoo amplified by the moisture. As good as nectar, drawing Celia closer and sending a rush of heat south to where only Celia's fingers and a vibrator had been in years.

"You two still going at it?" Chris's voice and trudging feet echoed from the stairs.

Helena unlocked their arms and stepped back to the edge of the mat. Bending, she grabbed the water bottles off the floor and tossed one to Celia. "You should put on a demo for Ethan," she said. "Pretty sure that'll slow him down."

"Not a bad idea." Celia cracked the lid on her bottle and took a long swallow, letting the cold water quell the heat that had flared between them.

Chris appeared from around the corner, quelling it further. "What's not a bad idea?"

"Making sure Ethan knows his girlfriend's mom can kick his ass."

"I like this plan." Chris's gaze swung from Helena to her as he pushed up his sleeves. "Want to show me what you've got?"

Celia wasn't a petite woman—both she and Chris had inherited their father's height, and she their mother's curves—but comparatively and objectively, Chris was massive. Ripped and trained, nowadays with experts far more skilled than her.

She cut a glance at Helena, who stared back at her like a proud, confident teacher. "You can take him."

Helena, of all people, would not blow smoke up her ass. If she thought Celia could take Chris, then she could. And if Celia could match up with Chris—hell, if she could even hold her own against her brother—then she had no doubt that when Dex reappeared, because he would, she could kick his ass right back out the door. With all the chaos of earlier, it was comforting to think she could at least protect her family from the danger they did know.

She screwed the cap on her bottle, dropped it on the floor, and stepped onto the mat. Confidence infused her movements and stance, helping her keep her limbs loose and at the ready. Like her teacher and friend had taught her.

Dark eyes clashed with dark eyes, and she raised an arm, curving up her fingers and egging her brother into making the first move. "Show me what *you've* got."

Helena howled with laughter behind them.

FIVE

Celia blinked once, twice, a third time. Didn't help. She took a giant gulp of coffee from her mug. Still didn't help. She closed her eyes and focused a good ten seconds on the sound of pouring rain on the other side of the garage door, then reopened them. Clear eyes and caffeine failed to change the sight in front of her or help her make any sense of it. "How the hell did this get here?"

"Holt." Chris circled the rear bumper of the black Charger parked in the Madigans' garage. A car that looked suspiciously like the one that had shot up the shop yesterday. "He was scanning traffic cams and surveillance footage for it all night. Found it abandoned in an alley in the Mission."

She drained the rest of her coffee, set the mug on the workbench that ran the length of the back wall, and pushed up the sleeves of her Henley. She approached the open passenger window and peeked inside. Everything looked in order, not even wet despite the monsoon outside. No broken glass, no torn seats, no missing electronics. No signs of prior life either. No change in the ashtray, no residue in the cup holders, no food or straw wrappers on the floorboards. The car smelled clean too, like it had been recently washed and detailed. "Abandoned? Are you sure?"

"Car was left unlocked, windows rolled down, tags removed."

"In the Mission?"

He tapped a gloved finger against the bottom corner of the windshield on the driver's side. "VIN's partially scraped off. Ditto the other VIN stickers."

"That's why no one touched it."

"Exactly."

"Okay, it was abandoned. Intentionally." Using the rubber band around her wrist, she yanked her hair into a topknot to match her brother's. "But why's it here?" She tapped the heel of her combat boot on the polished cement floor. "It's not wet, inside or out, so it's been here a while already." At least a few hours. "Shouldn't the cops be handling this?"

"It'll be back in the alley for the cops to find by midday."

She quirked a brow. "How's that legal?"

Chris offered her a pair of gloves. "Do you want me to answer that question?"

She was curious by nature, but she wasn't dumb. This was another of those Madigan-related limits. She could push—and Chris would answer—or she could leave it be. Did she *need* to know more in this case? Not for what she was fairly certain Chris needed her help with.

She lowered her brow and accepted the gloves, snapping them on. "We checking parts for ID?"

"Yep." Chris lifted the car's hood. "And anything else we can use to identify the owner or driver."

It had been years since she and Chris had worked on a car together, but they fell into it with ease, just like when they were teens working summers at the garage. Within an hour, the Charger's headlamps and taillights, brake pads, custom nose badge, and a dozen other parts were spread out on the workbench. Chris sat on one stool, examining each part and scribbling serial numbers on a notepad while Celia sat on the other stool, attaching the car's electronic control unit to the MaxiSys tool she'd retrieved from her SUV.

"A smarter criminal would have fried the electronics," she said. "Or wiped them."

"Means one of two things. Either they wanted us to find what's on there, or they were low-level thugs who didn't think that far ahead. The latter is better."

"Better?" Celia bobbled the ECU. "Helena and I were shot at."

"The latter scenarios mean *you* or the *shop* were the likely targets. Not Helena."

"I don't…" Words failed her.

"Fuck, that didn't come out right."

"You think?"

He put down the part he was handling and angled toward her, a foot braced on the bottom rung of her stool. "I don't want either of you to be shot at, but trust me, it's a much simpler situation if Helena wasn't the target."

She disconnected the MaxiSys, set the ECU aside, then hooked the MaxiSys to the separate tablet Holt had left for them on the workbench. "Meaning Dex or someone he's connected to. That's the simpler answer."

Chris nodded. "The more serial numbers I find"—he flipped over the nose badge—"the more likely that scenario becomes."

"What a fucking idiot." She ignored the gibberish flying across the tablet screen, assuming Holt would make sense of it, and picked up the nose badge, turning it end over end with her gloved fingers. "And what a fucking idiot I was for making that mistake too."

"You were young, Cee." She opened her mouth to protest—she wasn't young last summer when she'd foolishly considered giving Dex another chance... until he'd hauled off and hit her—but Chris spoke first. "And you weren't an idiot. Without Dex, we wouldn't have Mia and Marco, and let's not forget, he fooled us all and trapped *you* in a cycle of abuse that wasn't easy to break out of, but you did."

"With your help." It had been touch-and-go when Chris had first returned. She hadn't trusted he was back for good, and she'd still carried a truckload of misplaced guilt over the death of Chris's daughter ten years prior, but they'd talked, to each other and together in therapy, something they should have done a decade ago. Having her brother back in her and her kids' lives had helped make the final break from Dex possible.

"But *you* did it," Chris said, "and I'm so fucking proud of you." He catalogued the last part and laid down his pencil. "That's all of them."

She returned the nose badge to the parts collection and disconnected the MaxiSys from Holt's tablet, which had gone dark. "You could have just taken pictures of the serial numbers with this."

"Nah." He slapped his notepad against the edge of the workbench. "This will make Holt twitch more."

Laughing, they stood from their stools and began carrying parts back to the car.

"You're making better choices now," Chris said.

"What's that supposed to mean?"

"You know exactly what that's supposed to mean." He tilted his wobbly topknot toward the training room on the other side of the garage wall. "I know what I walked in on last night."

She snatched the wrench from him and got to work on the headlamp closest to where she stood. "Fucking PI."

Chris leaned a hip against the opposite fender. "Come on, Cee, spill."

She peeked through her lashes at her smirking brother, then lowered her gaze back to her task, feigning casual disinterest even as the fluttering started again in her stomach. "Nothing to tell," she said. "I've been legally single for less than a month, and if we're counting the years Dex and I dated, for the first time since high school. I'm not in a hurry to start anything. I'm focusing on the kids and the shop." That was her mantra, and she was sticking to it.

Chris, however, wasn't letting the idea go, seemingly intent on blowing her mantra to smithereens. "You're allowed to have a life too," he said. "You're allowed to move on."

"Like you did?" The words were out before she could stop them, and she regretted them immediately. "Shit, Chris, I'm sorry."

"It's fair." He pushed off the fender and began working on the opposite headlamp. "I didn't. For way too fucking long. I almost missed my chance because I was clinging to the past instead of reaching for the future."

She moved to lay a hand on his arm, then stopped herself short. The gloves weren't for keeping grease off her hands; that battle had been lost long ago. "I'm happy for you," she said with a smile, infusing it with all the warmth she normally would a hug. "And I'm happy to have you home again."

"Thank you. I'm happy too." He finished with the headlamp and moved to the taillights while she reattached the ECU. "And I don't mean to pressure you," he continued. "I just want the same happiness for you."

"With Helena?"

"She's one of the best people I know."

Celia poked her head out from under the hood to make sure it was still her brother back there.

"Snark notwithstanding," he added.

Now that was more like him. She chuckled as she finished reinstalling the ECU and closed the hood.

"Whether there's something there or not," Chris said, "she could use a friend, and I think you could too."

He wasn't wrong about that either. Her domestic violence counselor and support group had helped her recognize *all* the ways Dex had abused her, not just the one time with his fists, or the other instances of flying objects, but also the years of emotional manipulation, like isolating her from friends. She'd lost touch with classmates, despite living in the same town as many, and had avoided interacting with the school parents, not wanting to expose them to Dex for fear of what he might say or do to them or in front of the kids. She needed to start putting herself out there again, but she couldn't snap her fingers and wipe away a decade and a half of learned behavior.

Helena, though, was safe in that regard. She knew all about Celia's history and seemed more than capable of accepting and handling it. She was helping Celia handle it too.

"I think friends is a good place to start," she conceded.

"I'll take it." Chris said with a victorious smile.

Then an amused one as Mia's shout rang from upstairs "Mom! Come retrieve your evil spawn. He's talking over the *Bake Off* judges."

Celia wondered if her children bickered more lately because Marco was now officially a teen or because Chris was home and they were mimicking what they saw. Though Celia liked to think it was more banter than bicker between her and Chris these days. Case in point... "Are you sure Hawes is going to want to marry you after this weekend?"

Her brother's smile grew wider and he waggled his brows. "We get to run away to the condo at night."

"Lucky you." She retrieved the nose badge off the workbench. "As nice as this house is, I'm definitely looking forward to tomorrow's outing."

"Mom!" came another, more desperate shout.

"Go on." Chris closed the trunk and met her at the hood of the car. "I'll finish putting this back together and get it back where it belongs."

"Thank you for the advice." She handed him the nose badge. "And thank you for including me in this as much as you can."

"I know what it feels like to have no control." He

flipped the metal piece over in his hand. "And Helena was right, you're a better mechanic than me."

"She said that?"

"I was giving her shit for bringing the Duc to you." He shot her a smirk over his shoulder. "*After* I tuned it up last week."

"You did?"

"I did."

The hummingbird in Celia's belly soared, flying higher and faster on the heat that tripped through her veins.

SIX

Running late, Helena was hustling up the stairs when she nearly collided with Hawes on the second-floor landing. Years of training and coordinated maneuvers, however, made it so neither of them had to think twice about which way to move to avoid the other.

"Sorry I'm late," she said once the impromptu choreography was over. "I went into the office this morning to get matters sorted for a court call on Monday." She couldn't count on any spare time tomorrow, and God only knew what today's to-do list would look like after this debrief, so she'd had no choice but to hit the office first thing. The to-and-from usually didn't take long, especially on a Saturday morning when the city was slow to wake, but water falling from the sky doubled travel time, no matter what hour or day. "Traffic's a bitch with the rain."

"Same reason I'm late. Took me an extra twenty to get here from headquarters." Like their father had, Hawes often worked weekends at Madigan Cold Storage; easier to get work done without so many interruptions. He held an arm out toward the stairs for her to go first. "How are you doing?" he asked as they climbed. "Juggling everything?"

Vague, not like Hawes, king of the pointed questions, but she went along with it, assuming he was picking up the leading questions habit from Chris. "Pushed the operative meeting to Tuesday, so that's off my plate for now. Should be relatively straightforward, in any event. Recap of our contracts and some new recruitment targets. As for the day job, the other side's summary judgment motion was denied, so the case goes forward. The call on Monday morning is to set discovery and trial dates." They reached the third-floor landing, and she nodded the direction they were headed. "Which leaves this debrief. I gave Holt my lists before I left. I'm eager to see what he's found."

After two steps, she paused and rotated half-around, the silence behind her telling. "You coming?" she asked Hawes, who remained on the landing.

He leaned a shoulder against the wall instead. "That's all work stuff." A raised brow and Helena caught his meaning.

Pivoting fully, she rested a hip against the stair rail. "You're asking about Celia?"

He tilted his head, eyes twinkling with barely concealed mischief. Eyes that were icy blue like hers, like their father's had been, like their grandmother's. But the story in Hawes's eyes had changed. The ghosts that had long haunted them were gone. In their place was a calm and quiet assurance. He'd found where he fit, in the organization and in life, within the family and with Chris. Peace for the Prince of Killers, which left more room for humor and teasing.

She often played the role of imp, a sharp tongue one of

her best weapons, but she doubted levity reached her eyes like it did her brother's. Hers were closer to Hawes's eyes of old. She was happy with her roles, more settled in them day by day, but they didn't leave time for much else. Which was no doubt why Hawes was nosing around in her personal life.

But her life had no business being the center of attention. "Don't you think Celia's got enough on her plate? I don't want to make her life more complicated."

"So you *are* interested?"

She rolled her eyes and fell back on her old friend snark. "Fuck you and your fed."

"What?" Hawes said with a far from innocent shrug. "We Madigans thrive on chaos, including romantically."

"*Oooh...*" Helena drawled. "Is that what we're calling last summer?"

Red slashed across his sharp cheekbones, and Hawes hung his head, chuckling. "Turned out all right in the end." He raked a hand through his hair, then lifted his face. "I'm just saying, don't let the present chaos stop you from going after the good sort. And she is, Hena. We knew as much already, but having her and the rest of the Perris here..." His voice drifted off on a contagious smile. Helena felt it too. Their family home was alive again for the first time in months. Years, maybe. Full of the good kind of chaos. If they wanted more of that, they had to make sure the bad chaos was brought to an end. And to do so, she needed to put whatever she was feeling for Celia—the memory of last night's sparring session she'd replayed in her head countless times already—on the back burner and focus on keeping her and her family safe.

She restarted up the steps, tossing more snark over her

shoulder. "Since when are you the get-a-life tyrant? Especially *you*, who went out once in a blue moon to get your dick sucked before Mr. Hair showed up?"

He laughed softly. "I'm trying to keep you from making the same workaholic life choices I made."

A familiar gruff voice floated out from the computer speakers in the lair above. Proof of life Helena had to see. She hustled up the rest of the steps and into the room, Hawes on her heels. She nodded to Avery and Victoria across the room, to Chris in the command chair next to Holt, then pointed at the police chief onscreen. "He's worse than I am."

"At what?" Brax said.

"Being a workaholic."

The chief looked it too, more than ever. Hazel eyes bloodshot, skin too pale, wrinkles too deep, his hairline receded a little closer to where his aviators sat atop his head, and his normally square shoulders slumped under the standard issue SFPD rain gear. The umbrella wasn't doing much good either, the rain slanting sideways with the blowing wind.

"Push," Holt said. "I don't know who would win that one."

She ruffled her brother's overgrown hair, the ends starting to curl. His beard was equally scruffy, and she counted a half dozen used coffee mugs about the lair, two more than when she'd left this morning. "Or maybe you'd win, Little H?"

He swatted at her hand but didn't take his eyes off the man onscreen.

"You find the car?" Chris asked from Holt's other side.

"Right where an anonymous tipster said it would be."

Brax reversed the camera view, and there sat the Charger, in the Mission alleyway where Holt had had it towed from before dawn. "Doesn't look like it's been touched."

"I'm sure it hasn't," Helena said.

Brax swapped the view again, reappearing onscreen, his eyes narrowed. He turned his back to the other officers on the scene and lowered his voice. "If you've got the VIN and owner ID, send it through to Jax. It'll speed up our processes."

"Tit for tat, Brax," Helena said.

"You'll get the forensics report when I do. *Faster*, if I have a good place to start." He lowered the phone, disappearing from view and preparing to hang up, until Holt's urgent "Brax" stopped him.

He reappeared after a moment with his aviators on, unnecessary on a gray rainy day.

Hiding then. Curiouser and curiouser.

Holt leaned forward, fingertips on the edge of the screen as if he could reach through it. "Lily would like to spend some time with her godfather."

Brax's lips turned down and the divot between his brows deepened. Helena bet, behind those shades, the chief's eyes were closed. Pained. Holt's plea had hit its mark. It was well played, even if Helena knew it was only partially the truth. Holt missed his best friend too.

"I'll see what I can do," Brax said. "But things at the station are—"

"Busy, I know," Holt replied. "But—"

"I'll let you know when I see some daylight."

He ended the call, and Holt's wobbly "Brax" raked across Helena's heart, creating a tear she was sure was minuscule compared to the one opening in Holt's chest. For a man so big, he was eerily still, his grief palpable and heartbreaking.

"He's still pissed at us," Hawes said.

"Possibly," Helena replied.

They'd had to be more cautious than ever last summer about what information they shared with the chief, which left Brax on the outside more than usual, but it had been for his own protection as much as theirs. She hadn't been surprised at his anger over it then; she was surprised he was still holding on to it now. That wasn't like him. There had to be more to it for Brax to distance himself from the two people he loved most in the world. To distance himself from a promise he'd made to her six years ago and to Holt years before that. She scribbled another task onto her mental to-do list, then turned to the current crisis, a distraction Holt could also use.

She laid a hand on his shoulder. "What'd you find on the ECU?"

Holt cleared his throat and brought his fingers back to the keyboard in a flurry of keystrokes. "VIN number. The idiots tried to erase it elsewhere but did a half-ass job on the computer. Barely had to dig." Onscreen, he displayed the ECU readout and the photo of the partial Arizona plate. "Together with the plate, title tracks to Herman Mosley."

Helena did not expect the next picture that appeared: a death certificate. "He's dead?"

"Since last year, according to Maricopa County."

"So how'd his car get from Arizona to California?" Avery asked from where she rested next to Victoria against the other desk.

"I'll request the probate records," Helena said. "See who was supposed to inherit. Arizona is a closed-records state.

We shouldn't have been able to get this much." She squeezed Holt's shoulder. "Nice work."

"We're also running down parts," Chris said. "Two have recent serial numbers, according to the manufacturer. If Cee and I can track them to a shop here, we can see about getting receipts."

"And track who bought them," Hawes finished.

"I'll get all this over to Jax," Holt said. He logged into their encrypted private server and began uploading details for his hacker protégé inside SFPD. Jax would get the info to Brax, who would fast-track the forensics.

Helena crossed the room to her lieutenants. "Where are we on the lists?"

"I added a few names to yours." Avery tapped her index finger against the legal pad Helena had left for Holt. "Squirrelly fuckers from our meetings."

Helena read the three additional names. Two she agreed with but the third… "Frank Ferriello? You think?" The Madigans had taken out his brother, Nicky, last summer when Nicky had tried to take out Hawes, courtesy of their traitorous grandmother. Francis had assumed his brother's merc-in-charge mantel, and he'd been Helena's first road-show meeting. "I thought that meeting went well."

"Too eager to play ball," Avery said. "I don't buy it."

"And he's reached out to two of our soldiers in the past week," Victoria added. "He's fishing for something."

And that was why Helena had wanted the two of them read in on this. She could never catch everything, not with all the juggling, and Avery and Victoria were a formidable, dependable duo. Their deft handling of the details and the operatives allowed Helena to focus on the bigger picture, which was coming together in her head.

"Does our list intersect with Celia's?" she asked Chris.

"In three places." He spun halfway back to Holt. "Hit it, Little H." Chris narrated as three pictures filled the monitors. "Michael Griffin, Lenny Proctor, and Adrian Zima."

She didn't recognize any of them. "All low level?"

"Relatively. No one above soldier."

"Would explain the piss-poor evidence destruction," Hawes said. "Unless they wanted us to find it."

"That's what I told Cee."

"That car was awfully clean." Helena clicked her nails, contemplating the possibilities, but she needed more data to better assess them. "Give us the run down on the matches."

"The latter two are viable," Chris said, "Griffin, not so much."

Holt displayed a rap sheet. "Busted for felony murder. Built an explosive that was supposed to be for a B&E but triggered too early and killed two people. He's been locked up at San Quentin the past five years."

"How's he connected?" Hawes asked.

"Worked for one of the groups that picked up our explosives contracts."

A perfect example of why they were now out of that business.

"Associate at Oak's firm is listed as the attorney of record," Chris said.

"You're right," Helena said. "Probably not our perp, but worth a chat with Oak, if he'll do more than glare at me."

"He still pissed at us too?" Hawes said.

Helena held up her thumb and forefinger an inch apart. "Wee bit."

They'd hired Oak to represent Holt's ex-wife, Amelia,

who'd been caught up in Rose's plot. Despite the work he'd been cool toward Helena ever since she'd knocked him out in a stairwell while they'd been breaking Amelia out of jail. They'd promptly returned her—once Rose had been caught—but Oak admittedly had a right to be grumpy. Helena needed him to get over it for Celia's sake.

"I'll catch up with him on Monday," she said. "What about those two? Start with Lenny. I think I know where the other one is headed, and I don't want to go there yet."

Chris chuckled, effectively confirming her suspicion, but thankfully granting her requested reprieve. "We went to high school with Lenny. If Dex was into something, so was Lenny. Drugs, petty theft, you name it."

"He was on Celia's list?'

Chris nodded. "She never liked him."

"How does he intersect with us?" Hawes asked.

"He's Frank Ferriello's dealer," Holt said. Surveillance from Club Sterling flashed onscreen, the two men huddled in a booth, vials and cash exchanging hands. He zoomed in on one of the pictures. "Cocaine, by the look of it."

"Might explain the eager," Victoria said.

"Maybe." Avery tilted her head. "But I don't think that's all it was."

Helena tended to agree, which made this a doubly delicate situation. "If Frank is recruiting," she speculated, "would Lenny try moving up? Was the drive-by a test?"

"Could be," Hawes replied. "Nicky was shit at it. He fucked half his soldiers. Bred loyalty in some, resentment in most. There was as much in-fighting as there were skirmishes with the outside. Frank would need a new crop loyal to him."

"If Lenny's the best he can do," Chris said, "that's not much of an improvement."

"That's because the brains of the operation left years ago," Helena said.

Holt rotated half around in his chair. "You're talking about August."

Hawes's eyes flashed—the Prince of Killers among them —and Chris shifted in his seat, instantly in tune to the frosty change in his fiancé's mood.

"The older brother?" Chris asked.

"August made a better thief than a merc," Hawes replied. "He struck out on his own, using a nest egg he stole from us." He stood and moved to Chris's side, a hand on his shoulder to reassure, but Helena doubted Chris bought the forced smile any more than she did. "Let me see what I can find out," he said. "Before we go back to Frank."

Aiming to diffuse the brewing tension, Helena confronted the less than pleasant tension she'd avoided earlier. "And Zima?"

"Bratva," Holt confirmed.

Chris fully stretched his arm above his head. "Way above Dex's pay grade. I doubt the idiot even knows who he's dealing with."

"If Zima's low level enough," Avery said, "no reason Dex would."

"And certainly not Celia," Helena added. "Fuck."

"Make the call," Hawes said to Holt, then to her, "She was on your list."

"Remy Pak is always on my shit-could-go-sideways list." She curled her fingers into fists to keep them from reaching for knives that weren't at her side. Remy ran guns for the Russian mob, was neck deep in their business, and, after being busted by Chris in an ATF sting, a CI for the feds. And she was their go-between where the Bratva was concerned. "She's the definition of shit going sideways."

"Pinged her already," Holt said. "She'll be at Club Sterling tonight."

Fuck, and there went the rest of her day, because she wasn't going into a meeting with Remy Pak without all her bases covered. She'd hoped to spend some time with Celia, having missed her completely that morning, but it looked like she had an op to plan first.

"We need to talk about tomorrow," Hawes said.

Tension flowed the opposite direction, a tidal wave named Chris aimed directly at Hawes. "What about it?"

"Should we bring the cake tasting here?"

"It's a fair question," Helena added before Chris could drown her brother. "Frank is a loose cannon, and the Bratva are not to be fucked with. Not even by us."

Chris crossed his arms and slumped in his chair. "You want the family staying here until we have this sorted?"

"Stupid question."

"Then you gotta let Cee out, at least a little." Helena opened her mouth to object, and Chris pointed across the room at Avery and Victoria. "Put more operatives on us if you must, but we're going to AB's tomorrow."

"Are there cannoli?" Avery asked.

Chris smirked. "So many cannoli."

"I'm in."

"Me too," Victoria concurred.

"Traitors," Helena grumbled. "The whole fucking lot of you."

Hawes failed to contain his laughter. "You better call

your cousin," he said to Chris. "Put a few more names on the list."

"We're Italian. We always plan for extras."

Well, if the traitorous fucker wanted to lay down that kind of gauntlet, she had more than two operatives at her disposal. And all kidding aside, she'd use every fucking one of them to protect her family. "Don't tempt me, Mr. Hair."

The asshole grinned. "Do your worst, Blondie."

SEVEN

The front door opened, and a gust of cold air whistled through the mansion's foyer and into the kitchen, swirling around Celia's ankles where she sat in the built-in breakfast nook, two padded benches with a hand-carved table in between. She played a mental guessing game with herself: Who would appear around the corner? The house had been a whirlwind of activity all day, despite the stormy weather outside. She was happy to stay indoors, out of the wind and rain, but not the Madigans it seemed.

Disappointingly, through all the comings and goings, she'd only caught brief glimpses of Helena. A smile here, a parting wave there, in and out she went. Between their banter and the interrupted moment last night, Celia had been both excited and anxious to spend some time together today, had debated suggesting another training session so she could turn the kiss-fueled fantasies that had helped her get off in the shower last night into reality. She wanted to try that ankle move Helena had used, except Celia would use it to yank Helena closer and haul her leg over Celia's hip, bringing their bodies together so she could feel the heat and curves against her own.

But as the day had gone on, Celia grew more worried than curious—about her friend's seemingly breakneck pace and about being the cause of it. If Helena appeared around the corner, Celia had a mind to box her into the kitchen booth and make her take a breather.

But it was Chris who stepped into the dining room from the foyer, rain dripping from the ends of his hair and the tails of his leather duster. He strode toward the kitchen, and if Celia didn't already know something was up, if she didn't know her brother so well, she might have missed the moment, after Chris hung up his coat and tied back his hair, when he forced down his shoulders and wiped the wrinkles from his forehead. But she knew both things, and it was as if those wrinkles transplanted themselves inside her, creating uneasy waves of apprehension.

She tried to ignore them, focusing instead on her family, whole and safe here, thanks to the Madigans. Mia was curled in a blanket on the chaise in the glassed-in back patio, her e-reader and the cats in her lap, while Marco sat across from Celia working on his homework.

Until he caught sight of his uncle and slammed his textbook shut. "Uncle Dante! Where you been all day?"

"Had some work to take care of, then hunting down parts for your mom."

Parts she needed not for a repair but for answers. Using her connections, she'd tracked the serial numbers on the nose badge and brakes to two shops in the city. Chris had thought he'd have better luck getting the receipts for those parts, finding out who they'd been sold to, if he visited the shops in person. "You get them?" she asked.

"I did." The forehead wrinkles briefly reappeared, then smoothed out again as he came to stand next to Marco. "Whatcha working on?"

"English," Celia said. "If it wasn't obvious by how fast he slammed the book closed."

"I'm done," Marco squawked.

"With the grammar part." She eyed the paperback on the corner of the table. "You've still got a chapter to read."

"Suck it up, champ," Mia teased from the patio.

"We can't all be speed readers," Marco shouted back.

Behind them, at the kitchen island, Gloria clicked her tongue against her teeth. "You're cutting it close for dinner, Christopher. So is your soon-to-be husband."

Celia rested her chin in her hand, pressing her fingers against her lips to hold in her laughter. Another benefit of Chris's return, plus a new son-in-law... *not* being the primary focus of their mother's attention. God love her— Celia couldn't ask for a better mom—but sometimes the heaping helpings of Italian-Catholic guilt were too much to stomach alone.

Chris rounded the island and pecked Gloria's cheek. "He's on his way." He eyed her stained hands. "Should I warn him you murdered someone?"

Marco raised his own hands, palms and fingertips the same purple-red as his grandmother's. "I had nothing to do with it, Agent Perri. I swear."

Chris chuckled. "Evidence to the contrary, Plato."

"Beets." Gloria dug her fingers into the magenta ball of dough she was kneading. "A local farm box came today, and the beets looked amazing. I'm making fettuccine noodles."

"Murder pasta," came the voice Celia had wanted to

hear all day. Helena sauntered in from the kitchen's hallway entrance on the other side of the booth. "She got the recipe from Hawes."

"You two might be dangerous," Chris said to Gloria.

"No *might* about it." Helena circled around him and slipped into the booth beside Celia. "He's already made a list of all the pastas he wants to make with Mama Perri."

Chris patted his belly. "I see no problem with this."

"I don't either," Helena said. "So long as some of that pasta stays in the freezer here."

Celia nudged her shoulder. "If he doesn't share, I will."

Helena grinned, her smile chasing away any lingering chill in the air. It morphed into a smirk that she aimed at Chris. "I don't think you're needed here anymore."

Gloria laughed out loud, and across the table, Marco snapped his fingers with a hissed "Burn."

Chris thumped his head. "You done with your homework?"

"Yep."

Celia nudged the paperback. "Not all of it."

Chris picked up the book and held it out to Marco. "Why don't you take this out to the patio and read with your sister?"

"But I'd rather—"

"Let it go, bro," Mia shouted from the other room. She'd shifted on the chaise, turned half-toward them. "That's code for 'The adults need to chat.'"

Celia had figured her daughter's future involved copious amounts of flour. She was a gifted baker, as clear as it had been the day their cousin Angelica had first picked up a rolling pin. But moment's like this made Celia wonder if she'd follow in her uncle's investigator footsteps.

Marco grumbled a protest as he slid out of the booth.

"Fifteen minutes." Chris gave him a push toward the patio. "Then you can help with dinner and go back to avoiding Gilgamesh."

He raised his arms in victory. "Deal!"

"Not helping," Celia chided, then to Mia, "Make sure he reads the assigned chapter. Quiz him. I'm sure you remember the material."

Mia's dark eyes gleamed with older-sister delight, and Celia thought Marco might balk. Mia didn't give him a chance, pushing closed the French door before he could reverse out of the room.

"I like her," Helena said. "More and more every day."

Laughing, Chris grabbed two mugs from the drying rack next to the sink and the half-full coffee pot and brought them to the table. He topped off Celia's cup, filled his own and Helena's, then retrieved a bottle of Irish whiskey from one of the cabinets.

"News is that good, huh?" Celia asked as Chris poured a generous shot into each mug.

"Ma," Chris said. "You want to take a break?"

"I'm loving family weekend," she said as she continued to knead the pasta dough. "I've never had such a big kitchen to work in. But I know that's not all there is to it."

"There was an incident at the shop yesterday."

"I figured." She paused her work to glance at Helena. "Thank you for keeping her safe." Then to Chris, "And all of you for having us this weekend."

He tipped the bottle toward her. "You sure?"

She waved him off. "Get on with it."

"I see where you get the no-nonsense from," Helena

said, nudging Celia's shoulder. "And, Gloria, you're welcome to use our kitchen anytime."

"Oh, I plan too," she said with a wink.

Chris sank onto the bench Marco had vacated. "First," he aimed his gaze at Helena, "tell me about August Ferriello."

"I *knew* you couldn't let that go."

"Tell me why I should."

"He's not a threat," Helena said. "To you or the family. That's all you need to know."

Chris stared Helena down for another few seconds, and when she didn't flinch, he lowered his shoulders and shifted his gaze to Celia. "I got the receipts for the parts. It was Lenny who bought them."

"Of course it was Lenny." Celia braced her elbows on the table and raked her hands through her hair.

"The same Lenny you two went to school with?" Gloria asked.

"Yep," Chris answered. "Still worthless."

Celia clasped her hands behind her neck, gathering her hair into a ponytail. "I told Dex that guy was bad news."

A gentle yet reassuring hand landed on her back. "You put him on your list," Helena said. "General bad vibes or something specific?"

Celia closed her eyes and swayed lightly at the touch, letting it ground her as memories flitted through her mind. "There was always a bad vibe there." She opened her eyes again. "But last year he started skulking around the shop more, asking when Dex was gonna be back. I'd tell him never, but he didn't believe me. He knows Dex's MO too."

Helena removed her hand, and Celia instantly missed her touch. Shifting, Helena pulled out her phone, tapped the screen a few times, then laid the phone on the table in front of Celia. "Do you recognize him?" She stretched her arm across the top of the booth behind Celia. Boxing her in but comforting, unlike how Dex used to use the same position to intimidate her. "Was he ever with Lenny at the shop?"

Celia examined the picture of the dark-eyed, dark-haired, suited man. He looked like an extra straight out of *American Psycho*. Good thing for him the eighties were coming back in style. "Never seen him. Who is he?"

"His name's Francis Ferriello," Chris said. "Goes by Frank. Lenny's been hanging out with him lately. Not a good guy."

"Figures, if Lenny's hanging out with him. And the August you mentioned earlier, he's related to Frank?"

"Augustus, technically, but never call him that to his face." Helena swiped her finger across the screen. "Frank's estranged older brother."

Handsome, in a gruff sort of way. His brown eyes were a shade lighter than his brother's, his brown hair a shade darker and sprinkled with gray, and if Celia had to guess from the worn jeans and frayed Henley he wore, August hadn't donned a suit in years. Someone she'd remember. "I've never seen him either."

"You probably wouldn't anyway," Helena said. "He's a master thief. He's not doing his job right if you see him."

"Like an *Ocean's*-level thief?"

Helena smiled. "Better than."

"So not likely him yesterday?"

She shook her head and swiped her finger across the screen again. "What about this guy?" A shiver raced up Celia's spine, noticeable enough Helena again laid a hand on her back and slid her leg next to Celia's under the table. "You recognize him?"

Celia picked up the phone and peered at the man onscreen, making sure he was the same one she remembered. He was a bit older than them with a round face, beady black eyes, and blond hair. A striking, unsettling combination, especially with the naked malice that swirled in the stranger's dark gaze. In the picture and in Celia's memory of him. Same guy, and the same shiver Celia had experienced both times he'd visited the shop. "I didn't catch his name, which is why I didn't put him on my list."

"I added him," Chris said. "He and Dex crossed paths."

"He came by the shop—twice—with Lenny."

Chris jolted forward. "He was *with* Lenny?"

Celia nodded. "Who is he?"

Helena removed the phone from her shaking hand. "That's what I'm going to find out tonight."

Celia whipped her gaze to the side, worry cascading through her. "He's dangerous. I don't know how I know it, but I do."

Helena caught a stray tendril that had come loose from Celia's ponytail and tucked it behind her ear, her hand lingering close enough Celia could feel the warmth. It was a powerful antidote to the chilly words Helena spoke. "Good thing I am too."

EIGHT

"Mom! Emergency! HALP!"

Celia lifted her torso off the bench press and eyed her daughter standing at the opening to the basement gym. Mia looked a tired, bedraggled mess as she juggled her phone and the ends of the comforter wrapped around her shoulders.

"What's going on?" All had been quiet upstairs when she'd given up trying to sleep and had come downstairs to work out. She was too keyed up knowing Chris, Helena, and Hawes were out there doing something dangerous.

"Holt needs you," Mia said. "Lily's pitching a fit. I called up and offered to help but he said he could handle it." She cinched the comforter tighter and stared at the mats like she wanted to pass out right there. "Narrator, he can't. I tried to text you from upstairs."

Celia stood from the bench, checking the floor on either side and then the top of the mini fridge. No phone. "Sorry, I must have left my phone in the kitchen." She grabbed a towel and wiped down her face and arms. "He's all the way upstairs?"

Mia nodded. So Holt had wanted to keep Mia out of the lair—Celia would have to thank him—but he was also too worried to let Lily out of his sight. Or too busy to hand her off. Mom emergency was right.

Celia nudged Daisy off her hoodie on the floor, shrugged the sweater on, and zipped it. "Let's go," Celia said, giving Mia a gentle push up the stairs. Celia followed, Daisy at her heels. "Tell me what the crying sounded like."

"Kind of watery," Mia said, then made a gurgling noise. "Not her usual 'I'm hungry' or 'I want attention' cries."

They crested the stairs and ran directly into Tulip and Marco, the latter of whom was similarly wrinkled and bleary-eyed. "Make it stop," he groaned.

Celia ruffled her son's chaotic hair. "I'll get it sorted. You two go crash in the living room. The sofas should be big enough."

Mia wrapped an arm around her brother, turning him that direction, both cats trailing in their wake. "I don't know how Nonna sleeps through it."

Celia chuckled. "Lots of practice." Between her and Chris, then Mia and Marco, Gloria could tune out anything when she wanted to. Her kids, however, didn't yet have that skill. And she doubted Holt did either, which was not good when he needed to focus.

Instead of heading directly upstairs, Celia diverted to the kitchen. Given Lily's age and the sounds Mia had described, Celia had a good idea what the toddler's fussiness was about and how to hopefully make it better. She set the coffee to brew, pocketed her phone before she forgot it again, and washed her hands. She gathered a tray and the supplies she needed—a sippy cup of ice water, a mini-spoon shoved in a ramekin of ice cubes, and once the coffee maker began to drip, the holy bean water—two full mugs. Tray loaded, she carried it past the living room, checking on the kids who were settling down, then hustled up the stairs.

Celia was at the tip-top when Lily's gurgling cries erupted into a full-blown wail. She squirmed and wailed in the cradle of Holt's tattooed right arm, fighting the flannel he'd haphazardly swaddled her in. "Shh, shh, shh. I know, baby girl, I know," Holt said, struggling to calm her.

"Tag me in?" Celia said, and Holt's gaze shot up. He looked impossibly more ragged than he had last night, which, as she thought about it, was the last time she'd seen the middle Madigan. Maybe it was the pale skin or the ratty tee and ripped jeans making it all seem more stark, but Holt looked wrecked. "Mia said you might need an assist."

"I'm sorry if we woke them. I'm the only one here who can be *here*." He flicked a hand toward his wall of monitors. "She's so restless and fussy, and I've been trying to calm her, but I can't, and I need to keep an eye on the op, and—"

"Breathe, Holt."

"Can you stay, please?" The panic in his voice was unfamiliar on the quiet, typically confident giant, but it was familiar in her own memory, in her own voice, from those early days of parenthood. "She's never been this fussy before and not even my typing is working. I don't—"

"Ba-Ba!" Lily cried.

He propped his other elbow on the desk and rested his forehead in his hand, eyes pinched closed. "And Brax won't answer, and I can't…" The strangled sigh he made was misery personified.

Celia carefully pushed aside a keyboard, snagged the

towel off Holt's shoulder, and spread it on the desk. "Is she feverish?" she asked as she laid out her rescue tools.

"Last time I could check, she had a low-grade fever." He tucked the flannel around her again, trying to pin her flailing arms. "She's miserable, and nothing seems to work. I just want her to feel better."

"Ba-Ba! Ba-Ba!" Lily cried.

Pain slashed across Holt's features again, but with Lily's next cry, he shuttled it aside. "There's also a rash on her face."

The way Holt was holding Lily, Celia couldn't see her entire face, but she could guess at its location. "Right about here?" She pointed at the corner of her own mouth. "And more drool than usual?"

Holt nodded and surveyed the items she'd laid out. "What's all that?"

Celia pushed a mug of coffee his direction. "Reinforcements for us." Then gestured at the rest. "And teething reinforcements for her."

"She's been teething." Holt half rocked, half spun in the chair as Lily's cries escalated. "This is worse than usual."

"Some teeth are worse than others." Celia wiped her hands on the end of the towel, then swirled her right index finger in the ramekin of ice. With her other hand, she brushed the backs of her fingers over Lily's cheek. Warm, but not overly so. "You mind if I check?" she asked.

"Go for it." Holt shifted Lily in his arms so Celia could more easily reach her. "Though don't blame me if she bites."

"Kind of the point." Celia withdrew her cold finger from the ice and gently felt around inside Lily's mouth. "Mia was the same. Best baby, even at the start of teething. I thought I had it made. And then this one tooth, whoo-boy." Likewise with Lily, it seemed, the toddler clamping down on Celia's finger as it skirted over the nearly protruding tooth. "Yep, there it is."

Holt slumped in the chair. "Oh, thank fuck."

"Be careful." Celia shifted with them, resting a hip against the desk. "She's going to start picking up more words, including the naughty ones."

"Only because society says it's naughty. Between this family and a cop as a godfather, *that* word in particular is unavoidable. I'd rather she learn *when* to use it, not make it a forbidden fruit."

"Hmm, wonder if that approach would've worked with me and Chris?"

Holt arched a brow, and Celia was glad to see his dry sense of humor returning.

"Probably not," she agreed. "And I agree, it is a great word. So useful. But she's a little young to understand how and when to use it best."

"Fair point. Fuck." His eyes flared at the immediate slip, and he slapped a hand over his mouth, cursing behind it again.

Celia laughed. "We may need to think about a swear jar."

Holt laughed with her, more of his tension easing, until Chris's voice trickled out through the computer speakers. "Holt, you copy?"

Holt glanced over his shoulder, and Celia followed his line of sight. The image on one of the monitors resolved—Helena and Hawes in a booth at a restaurant or club. So that's where they were tonight. Part of Celia wanted to keep watching, wanted to know what danger they were walking into, but a bigger part of Celia knew this was something she wasn't supposed to know. Probably wouldn't want to. And an even bigger part of her was distracted by the screen to the far right, the image on it split between the shop and her mother's house that Celia and the kids had moved into last year. "You're monitoring the shop and house too?"

He nodded. "My techs wired the house first, then the shop once SFPD released the scene."

Jesus, that fast? Less than a day? How? She shook the questions out of her head. The answers would be information she didn't want or need. The shop and house were safe. That was enough. "Thank you." She tore her gaze from the monitors and focused on Lily, who, without Celia's finger in her mouth, had started to squirm again. "You need me to take her?"

"If you don't mind, just for a minute."

"Not at all." She cradled Lily in one arm, retrieved the sippy cup and ramekin with her free hand, and retreated to the seating area. She claimed the near end of the couch and offered Lily measured sips from the cup.

The rapid-fire typing and exchange between Holt, Chris, and several other voices, two she recognized as Avery and Victoria, a few others she didn't, continued for another few minutes before the activity quieted and Holt stood. Phone in hand, he joined them across the room, sitting on a chair arm. "That helps?" He jutted his chin toward the cup.

She removed the cup from Lily's lips and gave it a shake, the cubes inside rattling. "Ice in the water. Helps with the fever and the pain." She returned the cup to an eager Lily and jutted her chin toward the computer wall. "All good there?"

He wobbled his hand and opened his mouth, about to

say more, before he caught himself and pressed his lips shut.

"Should I go downstairs?" she asked.

"That's your call."

She shifted on the couch, putting her back to the screens. "Just tell me they're safe."

"Safe and with eyes on, Chris's included."

She covered her nerves by swapping out the cup for the spoon.

"Plus, they're meeting a contact we know," Holt added.

Celia focused on getting the spoon situated so Lily could bite down on the cold surface without causing further pain. "This is connected to what happened at the shop?"

"It is." Holt slid backward off the arm of the chair into the seat. "We're gonna figure it out, Cee."

"I don't like putting everyone in danger."

"You didn't."

"And I don't like causing all of you lost sleep."

Holt's chuckle was tired and resigned. "If it wasn't you, it'd be something else."

"So coffee is always an appropriate gift?" She'd reach out and squeeze his arm, try to offer more comfort than teasing words, if her own arms weren't full of adorable ginger munchkin.

"*Always.*"

"Are you usually here?" Celia asked, sweeping her gaze around the room, only lingering a second on the screen displaying Hawes and Helena. "When they're working?"

"Here or at one of my other control centers." He waved his phone hand at the massive wall of computers. "This is my job." Holt leaned forward, tickling the bottom of his daughter's foot. Lily made a happy giggle, a good sign.

"And her. And for other reasons." His gaze drifted out the window, then back. "We always try to keep one of us out of the line of fire." Celia couldn't hold back the flinch, and Holt rushed to clarify. "So to speak."

Before Celia could fret more over Holt's slip, a drowsy Lily mumbled "Ba-Ba" around the spoon, and the same pained look from earlier swept across Holt's face. Creased brow, downcast eyes, a shaky gasp. Celia thought he would ignore it, same as he mostly had last time, but his shoulders slumped on another shaky exhale. "Right after Da-Da, she started with Ba-Ba, and we thought she was asking for her bottle or blanket."

Same as Celia mistakenly had. "She's asking for the chief?"

Holt nodded and raked a hand through his hair, making a bigger mess of the reddish-blond waves.

"Where is—"

He dropped his arm and stood abruptly. "Give Helena a chance. You're good for her, and we all need someone." Celia didn't think he was only talking about his sister. "The change your brother has made in Hawes is unbelievable." Or only about his brother, but Celia didn't press.

"He's been good for Chris too," she said.

On cue, Chris's voice filled the room. "Holt, copy."

"Sounds like they're playing your tune again," Celia said as she removed the spoon from a snoozing Lily's mouth. "Go. I've got her."

"I'll put in my earbuds," he said. "You want ear plugs too?"

She shook her head. "I've got two teens and an Italian mother whose primary profession is gossip. I'm an expert at blocking out background noise." She tilted her head, lifting the ear angled toward the screens. "And I've got tinnitus in this ear from the shop noise. I won't hear as long as you've got yours in."

Holt clasped her shoulder as he smiled down at his sleeping daughter. "Thank you. I can't tell you how much."

She smiled up at him. "Been here, done this. I've got you."

As Holt returned to his command center, Celia snuggled farther into the corner of the couch, the snoozing baby in her arms calming her as well. So calm she almost missed the phone when it vibrated in her pocket. Careful not to wake Lily, she withdrew it and peeked at the screen.

All good here, read the text from Helena. **Get some rest. Will fill you in tomorrow morning.**

Celia was debating what to type back, finger hovering over the digital keypad—was "good luck" appropriate in these situations or was it better not to distract her at all?—when another text pinged. Not from Helena. She flipped back to the Messages screen and her stomach sank at seeing her ex-husband's name in bold, a new message from Dex waiting.

Ignoring it, Celia opened her text thread with Mia. **You guys good down there?** she asked.

Reply bubbles appeared, then a text. **Yep, Marco's already snoring.**

She laughed. **Get some rest**, she typed, giving Mia the same advice Helena had given her. **Might be up here longer than expected. Lily is teething and fussy.**

Aww, you're the mom-friend.

She rolled her eyes even though Mia couldn't see her and even though the sentiment filled her with warmth and happiness, same as the baby in her arms. **The snark,** she texted back.

Mia replied with **You're the best mom** and the kiss-face emoji.

But also the love. There was no shortage of it among her family these days, and she sensed it in the Madigans too. It just needed teasing out. Perris were good for teasing, as evidenced by her own daughter.

Kisses to Lily too, Mia added with more kiss-face emojis.

Celia pocketed her phone and let the rapid-fire typing behind her, her daughter's words, and the warm bundle of joy in her arms temper the need to peek over her shoulder at the Madigan onscreen she'd like to tease. If their lives would ever allow it.

NINE

Sitting in the center of the curved booth, Helena tapped her toe against the pole beneath the table, her motion in time with the thumping music and pulsing club lights bouncing off Club Sterling's abundance of chrome and glass. "I'm still surprised they let us back in here."

Beside her, Hawes sipped his whiskey. "We paid them well for the repairs and upgrades."

He wasn't wrong. After they'd put on a show of force here last summer, besting several other of the city's criminal elements, they'd become Club Sterling's patron saints. Repairs to the floors and furnishings and upgrades to the security and systems, which was why they were able to get those shots of Lenny and Frank. A small fortune, but worth it given the club's proximity to MCS. "And it's neutral ground now," she added. "Relatively." Another of the agreements she'd negotiated with allies and rivals.

Hawes lowered his glass. "That why Chris is at the bar?" He cut his eyes his fiancé's direction, then up at the mezzanine floor above the line of booths. "And Victoria and

Connor up there?" Then at the wall of floor-to-ceiling windows overlooking the Bay. "And Avery and Elisabeth outside on the boat?"

"Mr. Hair insisted." She tapped her nails against the side of her cocktail glass. "The rest are my concern."

"You don't trust Remy."

"Of course I don't, and neither do you. She's tight with the Russian mob and is a CI for the fucking ATF."

"Hey!" Chris grumbled over the comms.

"She cooperated last time," Hawes said, ignoring the former agent's protest. "How exactly did the New Year's Eve negotiations go with her?"

"Fine, until the part *after* negotiations when I wouldn't sleep with her."

Hawes choked on his whiskey. "What?"

"How'd that go over?" Chris asked, a smirk in his voice.

"She was miffed at first. Remy is not a woman who is used to hearing 'no.' But I bought her a bottle of Dom and got her the hot server's number. He'd been checking her out all night." Helena drained the rest of her gimlet. "And I told her I was off the market."

Hawes's brow lifted in sync with Chris's "Oh really?"

Rather than answer either of them, she flipped over her phone where it lay on the table. Still no reply to her text to Celia. She hoped that meant Celia was asleep. They'd had a good time over dinner, Hawes eventually arriving home and finishing the pasta dish with Gloria. Helena had even managed to get Holt to eat a plate while running over the op specs.

Just being at the club, though, should have cautioned her against texting Celia. The part of Helena that wanted to keep Celia safe and apart from all the swirling chaos remained strong. Despite Hawes's encouragement, Helena's instinct to protect, to withdraw, had welled up as the day went on, keeping her away for most of it, but the counter-instinct to get closer had brought her back to Celia's side at dinner, had led her to reach out in that text message, hoping for a response, hoping for fucking hope. She glanced again at the text thread, her insides aching at the nonresponse, then flipped the phone back over, screen side down on the table.

"She's here," Holt radioed. "Bay entry in three, two—"

The glass door in the wall of windows swung open, and Remy Pak entered alone, her smooth skin and long black hair a palette the club lights favored, accentuated by the little black dress that hugged her curves. Helena wondered where her weapons were; she always liked to pick up new tricks.

"Backup?" Hawes asked.

"She left one outside," Elisabeth radioed.

"The other is rounding the bar," Victoria added.

"Ballsy of her to enter before they cased it," Connor, a junior captain, said.

Avery chuckled. "That's got nothing to do with balls."

No, it didn't. It was all about confidence, or in Remy's case, arrogance. There was no denying she was a beautiful woman… and the second most deadly in the room tonight. She knew it. Probably thought she was the deadliest, but that was a cage match for another day.

Helena flicked her hair, knowing it would catch Remy's attention. Dark eyes shot their direction, then moved on, sweeping the entire club before landing back on their table. Satisfied, she wove through the crowd toward them, and over the comms, Chris hummed "Hungry Like the Wolf."

Helena glared at her brother. "Can we go back to the days when he was the enemy so I can kill him?"

Hawes laughed out loud, just as Remy reached their table. "Something funny?" she asked.

"Family squabbles," Hawes said.

"You Madigans do have a lot of those." She slid into the booth next to Helena, extending an arm behind her and scooting close. "You reconsider my offer?"

Helena made a mental note to check the collar of her shirt where Remy's fingers flitted, likely dropping a bug. "Good to see you too, Remy."

"Didn't expect it to be so soon." She glanced across the table at Hawes. "Where's your pet fed?"

A server appeared at the side of their table, a bottle of Stoli Elit and three shot glasses full on his tray. "From the gentleman at the bar."

He stepped out of the way enough for Chris to be visible, lifting his own shot of top-shelf vodka.

"I take it back," Helena said to Hawes. "We can keep him." She liked the ex-fed's humor much better when it wasn't directed at her.

"Happy to help solve that domestic," Remy said, having clearly caught on to the squabble. She claimed one of the glasses the server had left in the center of the table with the bottle. "You can invite him over."

"I like him there," Hawes said.

She tipped her glass Chris's direction, then threw back the shot. "His ass always did look good in jeans."

"And that ass is off the market too."

"Shame." She refilled her glass. "What about your brother? I hear he's available now."

Helena snagged a glass and pushed the other in front of

Hawes. "Chief of police might have something to say about that." Regardless of Holt and Brax's tiff, there was no way she or Brax would let Holt get tangled up with Remy. And it was good to remind Remy where they had connections.

"Greedy lot, you all." Remy sipped at her second shot. "So, if no one wants to have fun, let's get down to business. Why am I here?"

Hawes moved his shot out of the way and rested his suited forearms on the table. "What can you tell us about Adrian Zima?"

Remy lowered her glass and retracted her arm from behind Helena. "Tell your ex-fed I appreciated the vodka."

She moved, as if to exit, and beneath the table, Helena tipped up Remy's closest leg with her toe, then hooked the heel of her foot around Remy's calf, locking her in place. "Not so fast," Helena said. Remy's opposite arm went to her side, as if to draw a weapon, but Helena's arm was over her shoulders faster, a hand beneath her biceps, holding her limb out of reach. And bringing them close enough for Helena to whisper low, "There was a drive-by shooting yesterday. Someone shot at me and someone I care about. We're trying to determine the target, the shooter, and how to handle it."

"The person who took *you* off the market?"

It was a risk letting Remy in on the truth, but maybe also the only way to convince her how serious this was. "Yes."

Remy stopped fighting, and Helena was surprised to see the lick of fear in her eyes. "You better hope it's not Adrian targeting either of you."

"He scares you."

"Fuck yeah, he scares me."

"Because if he knew you were a CI for the ATF he'd kill you too?" Hawes said.

"Keep spinning your theories." She relaxed her battle stance, slouching into Helena's side, close enough to whisper, "Who else is listening?"

Meaning she was willing to talk, on certain conditions. Untangling herself, Helena downed her shot and reached for the bottle, discreetly lifting the coaster beneath it as she lifted the vodka. "Extra privacy," she said, explaining the metal strip underneath. She refilled her glass, then set the bottle back on the coaster.

Remy angled toward them, a sheet of glossy black hair obscuring the side of her face, preventing anyone from reading her lips. "Yeah, that," she said, answering Hawes's question. "And because Adrian is cold as ice."

"He's low level," Hawes said. "Just a soldier."

"Talk is he's angling to climb, and fast."

Meaning the drive-by could have been a test. Or a renegade move. "You took our regards to Dimitri and the Bratva?" Helena asked.

The Bratva were bigger than them. They'd picked off low-level thugs and associates, but never anyone above soldier. That would start a war, which, as good as they were, they could lose, and it would be a war with collateral damage. That was against their rules now, and they'd made certain promises—including to Brax—that they wouldn't bring that kind of war to San Francisco.

"We're in a good place," Helena said. "So are the Bratva as a result. They're no doubt profiting from our scale back."

"I did, and they are," Remy said. "They understand the terms."

"Would they order this anyway?" Hawes asked.

"A hit on you?" she said to Helena. "The queen?"

Helena suppressed her shiver and nodded.

"Order it, no. Object if it happened…" She shrugged.

Meaning *she* was the more likely target if Adrian did have a hand in this. Why else would he shoot up Perri Auto Works? Unless it had something to do with the other players potentially involved. She flipped over her phone again and pulled up a photo of Lenny. "You ever seen this guy around?"

Remy shook her head.

Helena swiped her finger across the screen to a picture of Dex. "What about him?"

She shook her head again.

"And you'd know?" Hawes asked.

"Seeing as I've been feeding the ATF the Bratva's recruitment targets the past year, yeah, I'd fucking know."

"How do we know you're not lying?"

"You don't." Remy reached for her forgotten shot and tossed it back. "But seeing as Adrian tried to kill someone important to me, I'd be happy to recruit you to *my* cause."

The pieces slotted into place. "The ATF thinks they're using you, but you're using them."

"No one fucks with what's mine." Remy looked positively smug, but behind the arrogance, something haunted lingered. Something they could use to their advantage.

"If we need a meet with your boss," Helena said, "can you make it happen?"

"You better be damn sure before you make that request."

"If we do," Hawes said, his voice and patience thinning, "we will be."

"And no one fucks with what's mine either," Helena

said, feeding Remy a little more of the truth in return for the truths she'd shared.

Remy poured herself and Helena another shot. "We understand each other," she said in Russian.

"We do," Helena replied in the same.

Remy's answering laugh was full and throaty. "Kiska, if I'd only known." She leaned closer, pushing back the hair Helena had tossed to get her attention earlier. "I would have tried harder to get you into my bed," she purred, unfurling a Russian accent Helena had never heard her use before. "Would have loved to hear you panting in my mother tongue."

A shadow fell over the table. "Just so you know," Chris said, "I've got a vested interest in this too. I won't hesitate to cause you trouble with the ATF if you double-cross us."

Remy's pleasant demeanor vanished. "I thought he wasn't listening."

"I wasn't," Chris replied. "But I knew what the plan was, and from where I stood, it looked like mission accomplished."

Some of Remy's fury mellowed in favor of annoyance. "You ruin all the fun." She shifted her glare to Hawes. "Are you sure you want to be stuck with him the rest of your life?"

Hawes drew Chris closer by a belt loop and grabbed his ass cheek. "I'm sure."

Remy smirked. "I bet you are." She slid out of the booth, taking the coaster with her. She tossed it on the floor and drove her stiletto into the center of it. "Just in case it was recording. I'll be in touch."

Helena waited for her to clear the door before speaking to Chris. "She's playing the ATF for her own purposes.

Your call whether to alert Tran." SAC Tran was Chris's former ATF boss who'd helped them last year. "I'd rather we not yet." Her gaze flicked to where Remy had disappeared into the dark night. "We may still need her."

"We'll monitor," Chris said. "You think she could be trying to start something?"

"Start it, no," Helena said. "Take advantage of the situation? She wouldn't object."

Hawes finally claimed his shot and tossed it back. "And shit just went sideways."

Helena didn't bother with her glass, drinking straight from the bottle instead. "Don't say I didn't warn you."

TEN

Head inside one of the bakery's three full-sized commercial-grade refrigerators, Celia stared at the shelves of plastic containers—quarts, pints, half-pints—and wondered how her cousin or Mia found anything. More than half the containers looked like they were filled with some sort of ricotta or mascarpone goodness. She closed the middle fridge and checked the one on the right. More of the same. The one on the left, nothing but liquids and eggs.

"Ang!" Celia shouted. "Where *exactly* is the cannoli filling you want?"

"Middle fridge," Angelica shouted back. "Second shelf. That's all the fillings. Grab the amaretto one too."

She let the heavy doors of the right—*wrong*—fridge swing closed and returned to the middle unit, staring again at the second shelf full of unmarked containers. "That's not helpful. Which one?"

"Why not all of them?"

Startling at the different, much closer voice, Celia spun on her heel to find Helena standing on the other side of the prep table. How the hell had she come in without making a sound? And how the hell did someone manage to look so good "dressed down" in jeans and an athletic hoodie? The snug teal top made her blue eyes pop and her blond hair shine where it curled over her shoulder in a loose ponytail. "I mean, we're tasting everything else in the place."

Celia closed the fridge and leaned back against it, letting the ambient chill cool her rapidly heating blood. "I'm sorry if this turned into more of a production than you all wanted." Between the sheer number of people—Chris and all of their immediate family, Angelica and her kids, all the Madigans and several of their colleagues—extra guards, if Celia had to guess, though she could tell they were also friends—and the sheer amount of food—at least a dozen cake samples and a full-scale Venetian dessert table—the bakery was packed. From the outside, the place did not look closed, and Angelica, with Victoria on her heel, was constantly greeting eager patrons at the door to tell them so. "We don't know how to do things halfway."

Helena rounded the near end of the prep table and her dark wash jeans did nothing to hide the subtle, attractive curves of her strong, petite frame. "My niece's hands are covered in jelly and frosting, so is Hawes's suit and Holt's flannel, and I think there's some in Chris's hair too. I'd say it's been an almost perfect day."

"Almost?"

"This is the first time we've talked." She pushed up her sleeves and rested against the table. "I'm sorry for that. Things were a little crazy yesterday."

"I'm sorry I didn't reply to your text," Celia said. Things had been hectic for Helena, but she'd taken the time to check in. Celia felt bad for not responding. "Lily was fussy, so I was helping Holt out." And she hadn't wanted to see anymore texts from Dex. None had been there this morning when she'd deleted the first. "How'd the meeting go last night?"

Helena curled her fingers around the edge of the table behind her. "More questions than answers. The usual."

"I'm sorry things got so complicated." She gestured at the rest of the bakery outside the kitchen doors. "And that this got complicated too."

"Jam-covered complications were exactly what we all needed today."

Celia laughed. "I'm glad we could help, then. We're going to be family soon. That's what family does."

Helena hung her head, chuckling too, though there was a sadness in it that made Celia's chest ache. "Give us some time to get used to it."

"You've got three weeks."

Helena's laugh that followed was lighter, and the tightness in Celia's chest eased with it. Helena straightened and pushed off the table. "I meant to tell you, good job on the car."

"Working on a car"—she wiggled her fingers—"felt good. Chris and I haven't done that together in a long time. I'm glad I could help."

Helena stepped forward and caught her fingers. "Thank you. I just wish—" In a rare moment of hesitation and second-guessing, Helena cut herself off and began to move back.

Celia curled her fingers around Helena's and held her close. "I get that there are lines, Helena, but—"

"Anywhere close to us is dangerous, Cee. *I'm* dangerous."

"I know, you told me as much last night." She stepped closer. "But your brother is marrying mine in three weeks, and your family is sitting in my family's bakery, covered in jelly and frosting. I think we're past that."

Helena's answering laugh was different than the previous two, and one Celia didn't think she'd ever heard from her. Soft, genuine, and a tad shy. She was surprised Helena had a shy bone in her body. "I like hearing you laugh."

Blue eyes peeked through burnished-gold lashes. "I like you."

Celia laced their fingers together more tightly. "Did you really tell someone you were off the market?"

Helena's wide-eyed gaze lifted the rest of the way. "You heard that?"

"No, Holt had on his headphones." She smiled. "He told me after."

"Fuck." More of that quiet soft laughter as Helena rested her forehead on Celia's shoulder. "They're ganging up on me now."

The sound and warmth, the intimate closeness of the touch, made Celia's stomach flip. "I like you too, Helena." She angled her face, feeling the strands of soft gold on her cheek and inhaling lavender-scented shampoo. "But full disclosure, I don't know what I'm doing here. Dex is the only…"

Helena drew back far enough to meet her gaze, and the rosy blush on her cheeks, highlighting her faint freckles, was another softness Celia had never imagined on such a sharp woman. "Doesn't matter how many or what gender when you like someone," Helena said. "And they like you back."

That was all the invitation, all the confirmation, all the borrowed confidence Celia needed to erase the distance between them. Mouth angled over Helena's, she moved her lips against Helena's slightly chapped ones, the soft and rough dichotomy the epitome of the woman she was kissing. Same as the cozy hoodie that covered hard muscle where Celia's hand landed on her hip, same as the sharp cheekbone under smooth skin where Celia's other hand cupped Helena's cheek. And as Celia teased open Helena's lips and dove inside, her taste was no different. Sharp, rich espresso contrasted with the sweetness of jam and frosting. Contradictions Celia could happily taste and touch all day. Could drown in as a whimper rolled up Helena's throat and escaped her lips, ghosting over Celia's tongue.

"Ma!" Mia shouted. "You get lost in there?"

Startled apart, Helena dropped her forehead on Celia's shoulder again and her body shook with gentle laughter.

"How do I tell them apart?" Celia called back. "Are there labels?"

"On the bottom."

"Got it. Be out in a few."

She nosed Helena's temple. "Who puts labels on the bottom?"

"Your daughter, apparently." Helena lifted her head, dragging her nose along Celia's jawbone and making her shiver. "She's smart, like you. I'm sure there's a reason."

"Should we go ask her?"

Helena grumbled an incoherent protest and dropped a light kiss on her chin. She stepped back and out of Celia's arms, but not so far as to break the connection they'd finally made.

Celia tangled their fingers again. "Thank you for that."

"Feeling's mutual." She lifted Celia's hand and kissed her knuckles. "Training tonight? I've got about ten pounds of cake to work off." And judging by the fire in her eyes, it wasn't only the cake she had a mind to work out.

"Sounds like a plan." Celia squeezed her hand, then released it, turning back to the fridge. "Help me carry these?" She didn't bother looking for the labels, just grabbed those she recognized as cannoli filling.

"All of them?" Helena said, eying the half dozen containers Celia lined up on the prep table.

"Doesn't matter how many or what flavor when you like them all, right?" She grinned. "Besides, Lily should get a feel for all the weapons at her disposal."

Helena laughed out loud, free and amused. "You Perris are good for this family."

"You Madigans are good for ours."

The doors swung open, and Celia spun to tell her daughter they were on their way, then stopped short at seeing her brother there instead with his work face on. "We're going to have to cut this short."

All the softness in the woman beside her vanished, Helena instantly on alert. "What's going on?"

"Brax just called. SFPD picked up Dex an hour ago. B&E and possession of a controlled substance."

Just as Celia predicted. Dex always came back. But the warm, firm hand on her back reassured her this time would be different.

ELEVEN

If Celia never saw the inside of SFPD headquarters again, it would be too soon. And yet, she was back in Brax's office, and once again, it was because of her deadbeat ex-husband. But true to Helena's word, Celia wasn't alone this time. The chief's office was packed. Victoria stood guard at the door, Helena sat beside her in the other visitor chair, and Hawes and Chris stood at either end of the chief's desk, following along as Jax, whose Mohawk was dyed a wintery blue, briefed them on the forensics report. Holt had wanted to join them in Hawes's place, but Lily had gotten fussy again after the busy day, and Celia suspected Helena wanted to corner Brax about the distance he was keeping from Holt and Lily. Tough, seeing as the chief's chair was the only one still empty.

"Anything else inside the Charger?" Chris asked.

"Nothing." Jax moved the crystal nameplate that oddly read *Captain* instead of *Chief* out of the way and spread a slew of pictures across the chief's desk. "Car was spick and span."

"It was that way when we found it too," Hawes said.

"Gloves," Helena said. "The inside of the car was shadowed Friday, but I could see the trigger, and I'm pretty certain the finger on it was gloved. I'd assume the driver was too."

Celia's stomach sank. She hadn't realized Helena had exposed herself that much.

"What about the parts?" Hawes said.

Jax's green eyes glanced up, directly at Celia, and Celia's stomach sank further. "Dex?"

They nodded and laid out a new set of pictures. Parts Celia had handled with Chris yesterday. "Prints on the parts traced back to Dex and Lenny Proctor."

"This and the receipts..." Chris rapped his knuckles on the desk. "That's the Lenny and Dex we know. Too stupid to cover their tracks."

"But why did they take all those other precautions," Celia said, "and not clean the parts or properly fry the electronics?" She kept coming back to the ECU.

Helena laid a hand on her knee. "That's what we're trying to figure out."

The door swung open behind them, the slatted blinds on the inset window rattling. Brax made it one step in before he lifted his head and stalled midstride, clearly surprised to find his office packed full.

His gaze darted to Chris. "You said you'd bring Celia down."

"Well, hello to you too, stranger," Helena drawled.

Brax's bloodshot gaze shot to her, searing, before he cast it aside. He quickly turned and closed the door, and from behind, his suit coat looked a size too big, hanging loose off his shoulders. Celia didn't think he'd bought it off the rack that way. He rotated back around and trudged to his desk. "You can't all be here."

"The person in custody concerns my family," Chris said.

"Which concerns our family," Hawes added.

"And I'm the family lawyer," Helena concluded. "Victoria is here because Celia and I were shot at two days ago, as you know. You really want to go ten rounds on this, Brax?"

Brax sank into his chair, and before Helena could start the next round, Celia laid a hand over hers where it still rested on her knee, hoping Helena would read the back-off message for what it was. If Holt looked a wreck, Brax looked like a ten-car pileup in rush hour on the freeway.

"Thanks for accommodating us, Chief," Celia said as calmly and as friendly as she could, aiming to de-escalate the rising tension in the room. "It's been a rough few days, and I feel safer with everyone here. If it doesn't work for you, though—"

He waved a dismissive hand. "It's fine, Ms. Perri."

"Celia, please, or Cee." She smiled. "We're family, yeah?"

He ran a shaking hand over his head and plastered on a tired smile. "Thanks for coming down."

"You picked up Dex?"

"Got a call from Holt," Brax said. "Dex was at the shop, trying to pick a lock to get in."

"I changed the locks."

"We changed them again yesterday," Victoria said.

She'd have to see about getting those new keys. Tomorrow Celia's problem. As for today... "Chris said there was a possession charge too?"

"Cocaine," Brax replied. "Enough I can hold him.

Longer if I can use this"—he jutted his chin at the evidence spread across his desk—"to make a trafficking charge stick."

"You'll get whatever evidence you need," Hawes said, his voice full of that frosty chill Celia couldn't put her finger on.

Brax glanced his direction, lips pressed together in a hard, thin line, before he shifted his focus back to Celia. "He said to call you for bail."

She laughed, not the least bit amused.

But it did draw a small genuine smile out of Brax. "That's what I thought."

"Thank you for calling, though."

"Arraignment?" Helena said from beside her.

The corners of his lips fell, and he plucked a gold-wrapped candy from the crystal bowl on the corner of his desk. "We'll book him tomorrow, pending charges, and hold him until the arraignment on Wednesday, unless somebody else posts his bail."

"Not likely," Chris said.

"But if someone does," Helena said, "give us a heads up."

"I'll do what I can."

"We need to talk to him."

"Interrogation Room One, but that box is half the size of this one." Brax lifted two fingers. "Two of you only."

Helena shifted toward her. "Your call whether you want to go in there with me."

Did she want to go into that room and tell her useless husband off? Tell him to leave her and their family out of whatever mess he'd gotten into? By all means. And for the first time in fifteen years, she believed she could walk into that room and do it. But did she think she'd be half as effective as Helena and Chris doing so? Not a chance. And this was too important to chance, too important to let her anger risk the safety of her loved ones. "You and Chris talk to him." She stood, and the rest of the room rose with her. "I'm going to go ahead and get back to Mom and the kids."

Helena followed her out from between the chairs. "Victoria will take you."

At the door, she glanced back over her shoulder. "Thank you, Chief."

"Of course," he said. "I'm sorry I broke up the party."

"Which you were invited to," Helena said.

Hand to her shoulder, Celia redirected her gaze and lowered her voice. "Go easy on him." At Helena's creased brow, Celia chuckled. "I meant Brax."

"No promises."

She leaned in and kissed Helena's cheek, right where her hand had been earlier, a reminder for them both. "Try harder."

TWELVE

Helena pretended not to notice the curious looks she and Chris garnered as they followed Brax around the outside of the bullpen toward the hall of interrogation rooms. After six years doing criminal defense work, thirty-plus years existing as a Madigan in San Francisco, and eighteen years since she'd thrown her first knife, she was used to the stares and glares from police, used to pretending she was any other attorney visiting a client at the station and not the target of periodic SFPD investigations. Folks didn't know what to make of her, a suspected criminal and a criminal defense attorney, or of the Madigans, pillars of the city and of its criminal underbelly. At least there weren't as many sets of eyeballs on them on a Sunday afternoon.

"You want to tell me what happened between you and Celia at the bakery?" Chris asked, distracting her from their audience.

Did she want to tell her future brother-in-law, the brother of the woman who'd seduced *her* this afternoon.

about the frosting-tinged kiss that had gone from sweet to heat with a single flick of Celia's talented tongue? "Nope."

"You want to tell Dex, though, don't you?" he said with a sideways grin.

Fucker knew her too well already. "I do," she confessed. "But I won't out her to that asshole. She deserves that satisfaction."

Chris chuckled as they turned the corner into the hall of interrogation rooms, and Helena was not surprised to see Hawes and Jax, who had not walked across the open bullpen with them, slip into the hallway from the stairwell at the other end.

Brax didn't seem the least bit surprised either. "I can buy you twenty minutes."

"Probably only need five," Helena said.

He opened the observation-side door for Hawes, who asked Brax, "You gonna watch too?"

"Fuck no."

Chris followed Hawes and Jax into the room, and Brax turned on his heel, back toward the bullpen. Helena caught up to him after a step, grasping his biceps. "After, I want a word."

"If I'm still here."

"Bullshit, we both know you'll still be here. Where else are you gonna go? Home alone." She used his arm to pull him far enough around to catch his gaze. "You made me a promise. You made *him* a promise."

"I'm fucking keeping it." The sudden vehemence in Brax's voice—more life than she'd seen in him in months—was enough of a surprise that she loosened her grasp, and he wrenched his arm free.

"You better be at the wedding," she called after his retreating back.

He rounded the corner, but she didn't suspect he went far. Whatever stick was up his ass, she knew he'd still protect them. Promises and all that.

She leaned in the observation room door. "You set?"

Jax was plugging what looked like a flash drive into the small control box by the observation window. "We're set."

Chris stole a kiss from his fiancé, then met Helena in the hallway. "Are *you* ready?"

"I don't want to be in there any longer than I have to be," she said, confessing another truth.

"You and me both."

Chris turned the knob on the interrogation room door and held it open for her to enter. Dexter Russo was handcuffed to the table, dressed in jeans and a T-shirt that hugged his muscular frame, his dark hair askew but in that way that on some guys was always sexy. Ditto the blue eyes, despite the bags he couldn't hide beneath them. Marco and Mia came by it honestly with two good-looking parents. She could see why Celia would have fancied him at first, before he got his hooks into her and showed her his evil side.

Just like the asshole he was, he barely took notice of her, swinging his faux big-dick energy Chris's direction instead. "Well, look who it is. The prodigal son returned."

"Dex."

"So Cee sends in her big brother to fight her battles now that you're back?"

"You're not worth her time." Helena leaned a hip against the edge of the table closest to him. "And I'm pretty sure she could kick your ass on her own just fine."

He glared at her. "Who are you?"

Chris mirrored her position at the other end of the table. "Don't play dumb, Dex."

He split a glance between them. "Why would I?"

Nothing in Dex's gaze indicated he recognized her, and the look she caught from Chris said he had read the same. He hadn't shown up for any of the divorce proceedings, which they'd both attended in case he had, so he hadn't seen her there. And apparently he hadn't seen her at the shop the other day, which meant he probably hadn't been in the Charger. And given his dick swinging, she didn't think Dex was smart enough to play dumb or that his ego would even allow it.

Chris grabbed the chair on Dex's other side, spun it around, and straddled it backward. "You been hanging out with Lenny lately?"

"Why's that any of your business?"

"What were you doing trying to break into the shop?" Chris countered, not taking the bait. Helena had to admit it was fun watching the investigator work.

"I left something there last time I was in town."

"There's a restraining order in place."

"That's why I went when Cee wasn't there, but the damn bitch changed the locks."

Helena grabbed the chains that held Dex's handcuffs to the table and yanked them forward. Dex's body lurched with the momentum, his chin smacking the table. She grasped the back of his neck, holding him facedown against the metal. "One, the restraining order applies to her person, home, or place of business. Two, next time you refer to her in a derogatory manner, your wrists will break and your teeth will wind up on the table. Do you understand?"

"You can't do this to me," Dex protested.

Chris grabbed him by the hair and angled his head in the direction of the camera above the observation window. "You see a light on up there?"

Dex's gulp was loud in the otherwise quiet room. "Fine, yes, I understand."

Chris released his head and Helena his neck, both stepping back. But neither went far, continuing to box Dex in, and Chris continued his interrogation. "Now, what were you doing with Lenny?"

"We're friends. Can't I just hang out with a friend?"

"You don't have friends, Dex. You think you can use everyone. But you're too stupid to realize you're the one being used half the time."

"You always were a self-righteous ass."

"I don't disagree," Helena said. "But I also don't think he's wrong. We've got your and Lenny's prints on car parts to prove it."

"Fine." Dex slumped in his chair. "He had a friend that needed some work done on a car, and I owed Lenny a favor."

"How many favors?" Chris asked.

Dex stared at his twiddling thumbs.

Helena tapped the leg of his chair with her toe and he nearly jumped out of it. "Fine! Fine!" Celia could *so* kick this weaselly fucker's ass. "Five figures or so."

"Christ, Dex," Chris cursed. "How'd you get that deep in debt with him?"

Helena wanted the answer to that question too, but she wanted the answer to another more. "Whose car was it?" Clearly it wasn't Lenny's, and after their chat with Remy last night, she'd bet money on it being Adrian—

"Mike Griffin's."

She would have lost that bet.

THIRTEEN

It was almost midnight by the time Helena returned home. After questioning Dex, she, Chris, and Hawes had made the short trip from SFPD headquarters to MCS to circle up with Holt, who Helena had strong-armed into skipping the station. She'd wanted to talk to Brax, alone. Fat lot of good that had done. Sure, she'd gotten an initial word with Brax, leveling a warning he'd nearly bitten her head off about, but he'd been "too busy" to talk again before she'd left.

The nugget of earlier worry continued to grow, her soft footfalls up the stairs like an ominous beat in the back of her mind—and in her heart. They needed the buffer Brax provided with SFPD and other law enforcement. More than that, they—Holt especially—needed the absent member of their family back. Her brother was spiraling. Fuck, she was surprised any of them were functioning after the last six months, but Hawes had Chris and she had too many balls in the air to think about the lack of a safety net beneath her high wire. Holt, though, only had Lily and his wall of screens. He was the best of them, the one with the biggest heart, and the recent losses and betrayals had cut him the deepest. She'd seen where that sort of pain could lead Holt, and she'd seen who'd led him out of it. She needed Brax back on board in case Holt found himself in a dark place again. If she had to kidnap the chief to force whatever confrontation those two needed to have, she'd fucking do it. Anything to make things better for Holt.

But at least for tonight, judging by the lack of sound from the floors above, Holt, who'd left MCS before her, was finally getting some much-needed sleep. In fact, the entire house was quiet, not a nosy cat—or nosy Perri—in sight. The nosiest had gone home with Hawes to their condo, and it seemed the ones left in the Madigan home were likewise asleep.

Loss of a different sort twisted through Helena. More missed opportunities where Celia was concerned. Against their better interests, she'd wanted to spend more time with Celia tonight, wanted a repeat of that delicious kiss from the bakery, and wanted to assure her that Dex was handled. She'd wanted the illusion of the safety net that seemed to appear below her whenever Celia was around. Comfort and quiet, even as the world spun like crazy around them.

The same simple comfort that wrapped itself around her at finding the Tiffany lamps in her room softly glowing, fresh flowers on her nightstand, and beside the vase, a cannoli on a paper napkin. She muffled a laugh with the back of her hand, not wanting to disrupt the quiet of the house and the quiet spreading through her. That washed over her completely as she stopped outside the open door of the darkened room next to hers and poked her head inside.

Greenish-yellow eyes blinked up at her from a tabby

face, Daisy tucked against a sleeping Celia's belly. Neither moved as Helena snuck inside the room and rested back against the wall to admire the beautiful moonlit woman whose dark hair fanned out over the pillow, whose sense of peace reached toward Helena.

"You're staring," Celia mumbled after a minute. Not asleep after all, or at least not fully. She hadn't opened her eyes, yet her assessment of Helena's presence and actions were spot on.

Helena didn't bother to hide the truth. "You're beautiful."

Celia's lips curved into a drowsy smile. "What time is it?"

"Almost midnight."

Dark eyes fluttered open as if fighting the weight of their lids. "What time's your court call tomorrow?"

"Eight."

She winced, the movement drawing a protest *meow* from Daisy. "You need to go to sleep."

"I will in a minute."

"Do you sleep?"

Helena held up a hand, thumb and forefinger an inch apart. "Wee bit. Law isn't the only thing they teach in law school."

Mention of the law seemed to wake Celia a measure more, even as she nestled more fully into her pillow. "Did Dex tell you anything useful?"

Helena repeated the motion. "Wee bit."

Celia chuffed, then unwound an arm from under the comforter and stretched out a hand toward her. Reaching toward her physically too. No way Helena could refuse that invitation. She pushed off the wall, crossed the room, and lowered herself onto the side of the bed. Daisy's death glare and Celia's drooping eyelids stopped her from doing more, but just this, just Celia's hand in hers, was the calmest she'd felt all day. Hell, since Friday. She hadn't been lying to Celia in the gym the other night about her internal monologue not being too far off from Celia's. Granted, hers was more concerned with Celia's safety than her own, but that didn't make the event any less alarming. If anything, it made it more so.

"Thank you," Celia said. "For dealing with him so I didn't have to."

Helena gave Celia's hand a gentle squeeze. "Anytime you want to tag me in to deal with that idiot, feel free."

"Not alone," Celia mumbled sleepily.

Helena repeated her promise from Friday. "Never again." She skimmed her thumb over Celia's knuckles, aiming to soothe her the rest of the way back to sleep.

But Celia's caretaker instincts fought the lure of slumber. "You need anything?"

"Nope, I'm good. Just wanted to say goodnight."

"That all you wanted?"

Helena chuckled. Maybe Celia was fighting some other instincts too, same as she was. She lifted Celia's hand and kissed the back of it. "No," she admitted. "But those plans flew out the window hours ago."

"And you have court in the morning."

"And you have kids to get to school." Celia's pout made Helena chuckle again. She added cute to the long mental list of adjectives she used to describe Celia Perri. This one near the top of her favorites. She tried not to think too hard about how she'd love to exist more often with Celia in this halfway land between sleep and wakefulness. "How's your day look tomorrow?" she asked. "Shop covered?"

Celia nodded against the pillow. "Yours?"

"Court, MCS, meeting with Oak."

A fond smile ghosted across Celia's face. "Tell him I said hello."

"I'll do that."

And then a blush streaked across Celia's cheeks, and when her eyes fluttered open again, there was a tiny flame of heat mixed with the drowsiness. "After? Another workout maybe?"

Helena didn't think self-defense was the only workout Celia was hinting at, and she was one hundred percent on board with that plan. "I'll see you then." She leaned forward and dropped a kiss on Celia's cheek, a mirror of the one Celia had given her at the station.

Celia purred, same as Daisy did when Helena gave her a parting scratch behind the ears. She stopped in the doorway, looking back at the cute, beautiful, amazing woman already asleep in the bed. Helena wished like hell there was a way to make this work because this sort of calm—this sort of peace—was something she'd never felt before.

FOURTEEN

Helena stared out the floor-to-ceiling windows of Oakland Ashe's downtown office. The lights of Alcatraz Island flickered on, earlier than usual owing to the storm clouds that hastened the winter dusk. Maybe the rain would let up tomorrow. She knew they needed it—California always did—but this was also about the time, every wet winter, when she'd had enough of it. And there were still a few months of rainy season to go.

Noise from outside the office drew Helena from the dreary view. "Oh, Mr. Ashe," said the legal assistant she'd met outside. "You have a visitor."

"I didn't think I had any other meetings on my calendar."

"Because," Helena said, voice raised, "I wasn't stupid enough to let you know I was coming."

"I'm sorry," Oak's assistant said. "She insisted."

"I'm sure she did." Oak pushed open the cracked door, and bemused gray eyes glared across the space at her.

She drummed her nails along the edge of his desk. "Fancy meeting you here."

He dropped his umbrella in the bucket just inside the office, hooked his raincoat on the back of the closed door, then crossed the room and dropped his briefcase in one of the visitor chairs. While not as tall as her brothers, Oak still towered over her barely five two. "Helena."

"Aww, Oak, you don't seem happy to see me."

"Not too keen on being assaulted again." He shrugged out of his suit jacket and tossed it in the chair on top of his briefcase.

"I'll play nice." She lifted a hand, pinky crooked. "Pinky swear."

He ignored the teasing offer, considering the offeror with narrowed eyes instead. "What do you want?"

"Guess there's a reason you're the best criminal defense attorney in town."

"You're admitting that?"

"You do have fifteen years on me, old man."

He finally cracked, a chuckle escaping, and she pushed away from the desk, strolling toward the round conference table in the opposite corner. "Need to talk about one of your firm's clients."

"You know I can't do that."

"Off the record. Call it a professional courtesy."

"I don't know that that's exactly what I'd call it."

"Privilege, then. It's a family matter."

"Conflict of interest." He circled the desk and grabbed two cut crystal glasses and the decanter off the credenza. "You shouldn't even be here."

"Well, seeing as your client, Michael Griffin, was in jail

at the time of a drive-by shooting on Friday, I don't think he did it, but someone is trying to make it look like he did."

"Okay, you've got my attention." He placed the glasses on the table and poured them both two fingers' worth of what her nose told her was high-dollar whiskey. She didn't begrudge him the drink, or the tie he loosened, or the sleeves he rolled up. He'd been in court all day, only to return and find her waiting in his office. "All right, out with it, then."

"Preliminaries." Helena lowered herself in the chair across from him. "How much do you want to know?"

"Privilege." He took a healthy swallow. Wise man. "I know your family's skeletons."

Or maybe she gave him too much credit. "You don't know the half of them." She sipped her whiskey. "Last chance to save yourself."

He drained his glass, refilled it, then tipped it toward her. "Go on."

"Don't say I didn't warn you."

She gave Oak the thirty-thousand-foot overview of the shooting on Friday, the evidence linking it to Griffin, and how Maricopa County had stonewalled her today on getting the probate information for Herman Mosley.

"I can help with the last bit," Oak said. "The title to the car came across my associate's desk after Mosley died. He was Griffin's last foster father before Griffin aged out of the system. Mosley left every one of his kids something."

"If Griffin was in jail, where'd the car go?"

"Storage unit in Bayview with the rest of his personal items."

"Who pays for that?"

"Ex-wife. Condition of the divorce."

Helena would have spit out her whiskey if she weren't already familiar with the hypocrisy of the law. There was a reason she did what she did—at both jobs. "He's the asshole in jail."

"I didn't make the community property rules." He sipped his second glass of whiskey more slowly. "It was either three hundred a month or half the other marital assets."

She sipped and stewed in silence, rearranging the evidence in her head, sure Oak was doing the same. "So assuming he wasn't suddenly out of jail—"

"Not that I'm aware of."

"Then someone else accessed the unit and the car."

"I'm guessing you want me to find out who," Oak said.

"I've got a few guesses, and if you give me the details, we can get the surveillance from the facility."

"Don't tell me your guesses. Let me see what I can get out of Griffin. As for the other..." He stood, ambled to the desk, and snagged a Post-it and pen from the fancy setup on his immaculately kept desk. He scribbled on the paper, then put his pen back in the holder and brought the neon pink note over to her. "That's the name and number of the facility."

"You remembered that?"

"There's a reason I'm the best criminal defense attorney in the city." He added a wink as he sank back into his chair.

She muffled her laugh in her glass, finishing her whiskey.

"How do you want to play this?" Oak asked. "I get this info, then I claim conflict and get removed?"

"No. I don't want us to lose control over this, but it's just you and me. Don't involve the associate who handled the case originally. Bratva could be involved."

"Fuck." He reached for the decanter again, offered her a refill, which she waved off, then refilled his own glass and took another healthy swallow.

"We all have to tread carefully." She wasn't only concerned about Oak and his legal associates. The more they learned about this case, the more Helena wondered if she'd made a mistake by rekindling her friendship with Celia, by letting Hawes's words provide the justification for falling into the kiss Celia had initiated yesterday, for visiting her when she'd arrived home, for tossing and turning the rest of the night as she considered following that amazing kiss and those softly spoken midnight words into something more than friendship. As much as her body and heart wanted to get tangled up with Celia Perri, her head was telling her that maybe she shouldn't have taken the bike to the shop. Maybe she should have let Mel continue to train Celia while she maintained her distance. Maybe Celia, Gloria, and the kids were safer without her in their lives. The Perris were already risking enough with Chris tied to the Madigans. Why should she double that risk?

"All right," Oak said, jarring her from her thoughts. "I'll find out what I can."

"We'll continue to gather evidence and organize on our end as well." She crossed one leg over the other and rested back in the chair. "And don't let on to Griffin about the Bratva. He may have no connection whatsoever, and prison walls have ears."

He nodded. "You think the Bratva are trying to start something?"

"Fuck, I hope not." She raised a brow. "Privilege?"

"Privilege," he confirmed.

"I don't think us or them would want to. We're in a good place, and so are the Bratva as a result of our scale back."

"Scale back?"

She considered her words carefully. She'd already stretched the bounds of privilege, which wouldn't prevent Oak from alerting law enforcement to future crimes. "Let's just say we're more discriminating in selecting our projects. As a result, our operations are narrower than they used to be."

He rolled his empty glass between his hands. "I realized things were changing. I just didn't know the extent."

"You looking for a career change?"

"Lord no." He pushed his glass to the center of the table, and his gaze strayed over her shoulder, staring out the window into the twilight. "I already had one heart attack. I don't need another."

"Oh, come on. Getting knocked out wasn't that bad. And I'm sorry."

His gray gaze swung back to her, amused. "While I appreciate the long overdue apology, I'm not talking about last July. I'm talking about ten years ago when I almost worked myself into an early grave."

She nearly choked on her whiskey. "For real?"

"I was a senior associate, second chairing firm cases and first chairing pro bono cases, trying to make partner and get all the trial experience I could while also taking care of a sick parent. I stopped taking care of myself in the process."

"Shit, Oak."

"Sound familiar?"

While the details weren't exactly the same, the stress load sounded eerily familiar. Multiple jobs, family obligations, all the juggling, all of it high stress. She'd never considered health reasons as something that would take her life at an early age. Those weren't the kinds of risk factors she dealt with on a daily basis. But that didn't mean they weren't there.

"The heart attack and my husband turned things around for me."

"You met him after?" Helena said, relieved not to be the center of attention again.

"He was my nurse."

Helena stretched a leg out under the table and nudged his shin. "Well played, Counselor."

Oak grinned, a rare, true thing, and it was like seeing a whole new person. "Do you have anyone, Helena, besides your brothers?" Except he wasn't. Oakland Ashe was still the too smart defense attorney who wouldn't let witnesses —or her—off the hook.

"You know how I don't want to bring an associate into this—" She waved a hand in front of her face, as all-encompassing a gesture for the Madigans as she could manage. "Well, a relationship would bring someone even closer. Too close already."

"Hawes made it work."

"Chris was law enforcement. He knew the score. He was inside, just in a different way."

"Ho—"

"Amelia was inside too, and so is Brax, similar to how Chris used to be, though he's been family even longer."

Oak *hmm*ed and made what Helena recognized as his problem-solving face. After a few seconds, he leaned forward, and with his index finger, drew a circle on the surface of the table. He traced a line from the circle's outer edge to the middle. "You're at the center now, correct?"

She nodded, confirming his deduction.

"Maybe you need something different." He lifted his hand and tapped a knuckle outside the imaginary circle. "Someone who's fully on the outside to balance things out."

Someone like Celia, who was fully outside, but also knew the score and seemed to have accepted it already where her brother was concerned. Who carried with her a sense of comfort and peace that Helena craved. But still... "It's too dangerous."

"I don't know." He relaxed back in his chair. "I think you could protect them."

She smiled, equal parts wistful and melancholy. "There is someone, but she's way out of my league." Celia juggled far better than her—the shop, kids, family—and she'd had to do so from such a young age. Hell, Helena had still been in her acting out phase when Celia became a mom. Granted, Helena was still grieving her parents' death, but the privilege and advantages she'd had were staggering in comparison. Celia had come so far, had so much to offer someone, and what did Helena have to offer other than snark and danger?

Oak's shoe nudged her shin. "I find that hard to believe."

"Are you a card-carrying member of the Helena fan club again?"

He chuckled as he straightened in his chair. "I haven't laminated it yet." He grabbed the whiskey bottle and poured them each another shot. "Why are you talking to me about this and not your brothers?"

She sloshed the amber liquid around in the glass. "Well, one's about to marry her brother and the other has his own crumbling relationship to deal with." She lifted the glass and tilted it toward him again. "And because you seem like a pretty strong tree."

FIFTEEN

Celia heard Helena coming a mile away. The angry roar of the Ducati pushed too hard, the screech of tires as she skidded the bike to a halt in the garage yard, heavy footballs splashing through parking lot puddles, short clipped words exchanged with Victoria outside the bay door. Then retreating footsteps in a different now familiar gait, Victoria's, the Ducati restarting and growling as Victoria exited the lot on it. Finally, two slaps against the gate and door button. All that racket, caused by someone who had snuck up on her yesterday without a peep, meant two things: Helena wanted Celia to know she was there, and she wanted her to know she was hella pissed.

Celia rolled her head on the dolly's padded headrest, eyeing a pair of black leather boots spread shoulder width apart at the rear of the Bentley. Racket and movement beyond Helena's feet drew Celia's attention to the yard where the flood lights reflected off the newly lined metal gate rolling closed. Seconds later, the clanking bay door cut off Celia's view of the dark, drippy outdoors entirely.

"What the fuck are you doing here, Celia?" Oh, not even a *Cee*. Helena's words were as sharp and angry as her movements. Nothing like the softness and warmth of yesterday. Cold even, like Celia had heard in Hawes's voice at the station, but that wasn't all there was in Helena's. It was more like a cold front holding back the heat, like the last gasp of foggy midsummer in the city before late summer arrived with a triple degree heatwave. Fire simmered beneath Helena's clipped question.

A fire Celia had knowingly put there. She wasn't a fool. She knew coming to the garage would piss Helena off, yet she'd done it anyway. She couldn't magically reverse the last two hours, and she wouldn't even if she could. She cringed at the wrath she'd wrought, but she wasn't going to back down. In for a penny, in for a pound. "What's it look like I'm doing? And that's five dollars to the swear jar."

"You're responsible for that?"

"I am."

"Good, we need all the help we can get there. And I thought you said you had all the help you needed to cover here today."

She rolled her face away from Helena's feet, focusing on the underbody above her, and finished the checks on the Bentley. "I did."

Helena stalked from the back of the car to the driver's side, closer to where Celia was wheeled under. "Then why are you here?"

"Because I promised Bill his Bentley tomorrow, and I needed to do the final checks."

"Lorenzo couldn't do it?"

She tightened the last bolt and rolled out from under the sedan. Directly between Helena's spread legs. She stared up at the fetching woman in dark denim, blue cashmere, and a rain-dappled leather duster. With her blond hair and fiery blue eyes, she looked like an avenging angel. The sexiest one Celia had ever seen, and it only made her want to draw Helena closer, fire be damned.

"It's my name on this shop." She pointed with a wrench to the roof near the front of the shop where Perri Auto Works was installed on the fascia outside. "It's my reputation, my family's reputation and livelihood, and the livelihood of everyone who works for me."

Helena flicked out the ends of her coat and shoved aside the lapels so she could plant her hands on her hips, one of them cocked. Oh, she was mad, and fucking gorgeous. "None of which will matter if you wind up dead."

"Victoria was on guard."

"That's not the point, Cee."

Celia felt a little remorse for the worry that seeped into Helena's voice, but she wasn't done making *her* point. "No, it wasn't." She set the wrench aside, wiped her hands on the shop rag in the pocket of her coveralls, and levered up onto her elbows. "You want to know why I'm here?"

Helena ditched her jacket altogether, jerking it off and hurling it onto a stack of tires. She lowered into a crouch, holding herself inches above Celia's middle. "Can't wait to hear this one."

If the heat had been simmering before, it was boiling now, and flowing directly Celia's direction, ratcheting up the pulse pounding between her legs. She was past the point of no return, and she had no intention of turning back. The hummingbirds in her stomach were going wild, spinning and fluttering, but at this point, Celia didn't see a way to calm them other than to feed them, and the best shot at doing that was to give Helena the pure unvarnished truth. "Because after spending all day knocking around *your* house, wondering what it would be like to kiss you in this room or that, I had to get out of there."

What little frost remained melted away, Helena's smirk and her crouch deepening. She braced her forearms on her knees and leaned her torso more fully over Celia's. "You could have gone to your house. We've cleared it. All the security is set up, and you'd have guards."

"But then I'd just wonder what it would be like to kiss you there."

Helena's blue eyes flashed icy hot and the corner of her mouth hitched higher. Celia wanted to lunge up and capture those twisted lips, wanted another taste of the woman she couldn't get out of her mind, sure the flavors would be different yet no less amazing today. But before she could make her move, Helena grasped the zipper tab of her coveralls and slid it down. She let her fingers linger above where Celia wanted them most, and Celia bit back a gasp, the boiling heat inside her barreling south on a tidal wave of lust. "For someone who's only dated one other person, you're awfully good at this flirting thing."

"Have you met my brother?"

"Let's not bring him into this."

She gently clasped Helena's knees and tugged. "Admit it, you like him."

Following her cue, Helena lowered one then the other knee onto the garage floor on either side of her, bringing their bodies into direct contact. "Not as much as I like you."

"Thank goodness for that." Celia was dying to thrust up, aching for friction and the warmth she could feel through layers of clothing. As if reading her mind, or just wanting the same as much as she did, Helena braced a hand on the door of the Bentley and canted her hips.

The roll of the dolly made it both better and worse. Better in that Celia moved effortlessly with Helena. Worse in that she needed to move against Helena's body for the friction she desperately craved. Celia bent her knees, planted her feet firmly on the ground, and tried again. Better, but... She coasted her hands up Helena's thighs and grasped her hips, holding her exactly where she needed her. She rolled up and... oh, what sweet relief. Not everything she wanted, but better.

Not enough for Helena though, who snuck a hand inside Celia's coveralls and with her thumb, teased the side of Celia's breast through her tank and bra. Her other fingertips were soft and cool against Celia's underarm, exposed by the sleeveless tank. Celia shivered, her eyes fluttering closed, her breaths coming shorter. It had been years since anyone had touched her so gently, so intimately. Helena's hand drifted down, then back up, under Celia's tank, gliding across her overheated skin. Those same cool fingers splayed over her ribs, Helena's thumb and forefinger framing the underside of Celia's breast. The light squeeze made Celia gasp again and open her eyes.

Helena grinned, wicked and gorgeous, and wetness joined the pounding heat between Celia's thighs. Helena rolled her hips again, and Celia wondered if she could feel the dampness, if Helena was as turned on as she was. "So you came here to not think about me?"

"No." She lifted a hand off Helena's hip and raked it through the blond hair that cascaded around them like a curtain. "I came here so I could put my hands on something besides my—"

Helena came down fully on top of her—lips, hands, body—and fuck yeah, Helena was as turned on as she was. If yesterday's kiss had been sweet tinged with heat, this one was heat tinged with overwhelming hunger. Nothing sweet about it on either of their parts. Celia parted her lips and Helena plundered her mouth, sweeping in and over teeth and tongue. Celia groaned, loving the slide of Helena's tongue almost as much as she loved the slide of Helena's hand fully onto her breast, cupping and squeezing it, thumb teasing her nipple. Almost as much as she loved the slide of Helena's other hand down her torso and inside the bottom of her coveralls.

Helena cupped her between her legs, over the yoga pants Celia had on under her coveralls. "How about *I* put my hands on it instead?"

Celia rocked into the touch. "That's a start."

"You're right. It's a start." Helena kissed a path over her chin and neck and pressed more firmly with her hand, the heel of her palm applying delicious pressure on Celia's clit, her fingers teasing her labia through the thin fabric. No way she could miss the wetness now, the crotch of Celia's pants and barely there thong becoming more drenched by the second. "My fingers, gliding through all that wetness." Oh yeah, she knew… and aimed to make it worse. "My thumb torturing your clit, as the rest of my fingers sink deep inside you." She shifted her hand and her thumb landed right on its target, circling in time with the thumb rolling her nipple.

Groaning, Celia arched into Helena's touch. "I'm good with all that." Rocked again in case she wasn't clear. "Please."

"Problem is…" Helena kissed across her chest and licked beneath the boatneck of her tank, hinting at where her tongue might go. "You're on a dolly, and you're too fucking tall. I can't spread you out in all your beautiful fucking glory here."

If Celia had been standing, she would have swooned. As it were, another wave of heat and wetness arrowed south, and as much as she wanted to use her hand still in Helena's hair to direct her mouth over her nipple or over her pussy. Helena was right. There wasn't enough room here. And she wanted to get her hands and mouth on more of Helena too. "Couch," she panted. "In my office."

There was a moment of bereft chill, Helena's lips, hands, and weight lifting off her body, but then Helena was hauling Celia up by both arms and bringing their lips back together.

"Someone's in a hurry," Celia teased against Helena's lips.

Helena nipped her bottom one. "Your hot and soaked for me, and I'm the same for you." She took one of Celia's hands in hers and shoved it against her pussy, and fuck, even through the denim, Celia felt the heat and dampness. "I've been this way since Friday. Fuck, longer. I was trying to stay away, trying to keep you safe, but I want you. I've wanted you since I first laid eyes on you."

"You're gonna owe so much money to the swear jar after this," Celia muttered as they staggered into the neighboring bay. She shrugged the rest of the way out of the top of her coveralls, and as soon as the garment fell around her waist, Helena grabbed the hem of her tank and yanked it up and off. She expected Helena's mouth to collide again with hers, but instead it landed on the swell of her right breast, warm breath and a wet tongue teasing Celia through black lace. Knees weak, Celia flung out a hand and caught herself on the hood of the SS. Taking full advantage, Helena caught both her wrists and held them wide, exposing all of Celia's front to her mouth. She kissed and licked a path from one breast to the other, sucking each nipple through the lace cups, the heat and friction bringing Celia close to the edge.

Celia wanted to vault up onto the hood of the Chevelle and throw her legs over Helena's hips. Or better yet, splay herself out on it, but there had to be some limits. "This is Whiskey Walker's SS," she managed between gasps. "We can't fuck on the hood."

Helena shoved a thigh between her legs, pressing up against her aching center. "He's a friend. He'll understand."

"This might be a bridge too far." Celia bore down on Helena's thigh, chasing the friction, even as she tugged against the hands around her wrists. "And I want to touch you too."

That was enough to get Helena moving again, and after a few more heated moments—against the sink where Celia quickly washed up, Helena's hands dancing all over her as she did; against the door to the interior part of the garage where Celia rid Helena of her sweater and got her first sight of pert porcelain breasts encased in blue satin and her first taste of soft lavender-scented skin above the satin cups; and against the hallway wall outside Celia's office where Helena slipped her hands inside the back of Celia's pants and dug her nails into Celia's ass cheeks, eliciting a deep and hungry groan—they finally made it into Celia's office. Where the hottest moment yet found Celia facing her desk as Helena finished stripping her out of her coveralls.

Celia expected to turn around and finish stripping Helena too, to stumble over to the couch against the far wall and tangle their limbs together, but before Celia could do any of that, before she could even catch her breath, Helena glided a hand over her hip and inside her pants.

She stopped halfway to where Celia wanted her touch most. "You been tested recently?"

Celia nodded. "I'm okay. You?"

"I'm good too. Now, where was I..." She dipped her hand lower, shoved aside the thong, and slid two fingers between her slick folds on either side of her clit.

A direct indirect hit that stole Celia's breath.

"Fuck, Cee," Helena mouthed against the back of her shoulder. "You feel so good." Her other hand cupped Celia's breast holding her upright. Holding her exposed. She hadn't let herself be this open, this vulnerable, with Dex in at least a decade. Feared it even. But with Helena, she'd never felt so wanted or sexy.

Or safe.

She covered Helena's hand over her breast and squeezed, the fact they were fondling her together ramping her higher. "You feel good too. Wanna feel more."

Helena released her, but Celia was too hot to feel a chill this time, and she trusted Helena would be right there when she turned around. The sight that greeted her was even better—Helena unbuttoning and lowering her jeans, revealing satin underwear that matched the blue of her bra. Celia moved to lower her pants too, but Helena stopped her. "No, leave them on. You in that bra and those tight-ass pants is incredibly sexy."

"But there's a thong under here," Celia muttered against her lips as they edged toward the couch.

"I know. Fucking lace. Does it match the bra?"

Celia smiled.

Growling, Helena gave her a light shove and Celia fell

into the couch cushions. "If I see that," Helena said as she lowered her weight onto Celia's thighs, "I won't be able to stop myself, and the first time I eat you out, I want it to be on a bed where I can spread you out on cotton sheets and fucking feast."

Celia's eyes fluttered closed and she dropped her head back on the cushions, the image Helena had put in her mind too erotic to bear. "Holy fuck. I'd always thought about the gym mats, but that works too."

Helena dragged a damp finger up her neck to her chin, drawing Celia's gaze back upright. "Look what you do to me, Cee." Her eyes flicked down, and Celia followed her gaze. With Helena straddling her, legs spread, her soaked satin underwear were on full display. She hadn't been lying, and Celia felt her own swell of pride. She'd done that. After years of being told she was no longer sexy, no longer attractive, that she was used up and not worth the time anymore, the sexiest person she knew was straddled across her thighs and soaking wet. For her.

"Yeah, baby," Helena said. "You did that." She inched the tip of her finger between Celia's parted lips. The flavor on Helena's fingertip was sharp and musky, with only the faintest scent of lavender. Celia had no doubt Helena had touched herself while Celia's eyes had been closed and now she was tasting Helena on her tongue, and fuck did she want more of that, but she wanted to touch first.

She reached a hand toward Helena's underwear, then hesitated, suddenly shy and nervous. She'd never done this before with anyone but a man, and only one man at that.

"You know exactly what to do." Helena leaned forward and gave her an encouraging kiss. "You know what feels good." She put her hand down Celia's pants again, moved aside the thong, and nestled her fingers between her folds.

Celia mimicked the motion, pushing Helena's briefs aside and gliding the tips of her fingers through short coarse hairs on the way to warm enticing wetness. "Oh fuck. Helena that feels…"

"So good," Helena groaned. She rolled her hips and rode Celia's fingers, creating her own friction and giving Celia an even better tour of her hot, slick pussy.

Celia sank farther into the cushions, canting her hips and drawing Helena closer. Helena braced a hand behind her on the back of the couch, and Celia cupped her breast. The weight in her hand was perfect as were the goosebumps that rose on Helena's skin. Wanting to feel and see more, she dipped her fingers into the cup and lifted out her breast.

"Pinch it," Helena said.

Celia rolled the rosy nipple between her thumb and forefinger, then pinched, and Helena's back bowed. More wetness covered Celia's fingers where they continued to slide between Helena's labia. She followed the source of heat and her own curiosity and desire and sank a finger inside Helena.

So hot, so tight, and Helena made it more so, clenching her muscles. "That's it, Cee. Fuck me."

She pumped one, then two fingers inside Helena, faltering momentarily as Helena sank two fingers inside her. It only took a couple seconds for them to get into a rhythm together, the roll of their hips and their touches in sync.

Celia drew back enough to admire the woman astride her lap. Her strong body, the attractive blush spread across her porcelain skin, the beads of sweat that dotted her hairline, all that sex-tousled hair.

"Like what you see?"

Celia's gaze returned to Helena's lust-darkened one. "Yeah, I like it a lot."

"You know what I want to see?"

"What's that?" Celia panted.

"You come." Helena thrust her fingers inside Celia, once, twice more, then dragged them up to circle her clit. Once, twice again, then she pressed directly against the aching bundle of nerves. Celia shouted as her orgasm ripped through her, shocks of heat and pleasure pulsing from her center all the way out to her fingers and toes.

Including the ones inside Helena, whose muscles fluttered around them. She was on the same cliff Celia had just toppled over, and Celia wanted Helena there with her in the pleasurable afterglow. Angling her thumb, she found Helena's clit and gave it a few rough passes.

Helena bucked hard and dropped her forehead onto Celia's shoulder. "Almost there," she panted. "Make me come, Cee."

Celia curled the fingers inside her and swiped her thumb once more over Helena's clit. That was all it took. Helena rode out her orgasm with her teeth lightly biting Celia's shoulder.

Celia knew it was over when teeth became lips, gently kissing across her collarbone until Helena was nuzzling the crook of her neck. Who would have thought Helena Madigan was a cuddler? Celia angled her head, likewise nuzzling Helena's temple. "Thank you," Celia whispered. "That was the best orgasm I've had since I can't remember when. Maybe ever."

Helena chuffed and lolled her head on Celia's shoulder, glancing up at her through the errant blond strands that fell across her face. It was the single hottest look that had ever been cast Celia's way. And the words that followed only ramped up the temperature. "Oh, baby, we're just getting started."

SIXTEEN

Helena darkened her tablet screen, which in turn darkened the projection screen at the front of the conference room where she stood. To her right, Avery hit the switch to deactivate the blackout glass on the interior and exterior windows, letting back in the soft light of MCS's executive floor and the muted gray of another rainy January day.

Helena set her tablet on the end of the conference table and tugged the lapels of her leather jacket closed, buffering against the imaginary winter chill the gloomy outside brought. "That's the current slate of contracts," she said to the gathered captains and lieutenants. "Everyone clear on marching orders?"

The operatives nodded, a few absently as they continued to scroll through the more detailed assignments on their individual tablets.

"It's good work, boss," Avery said.

"She's right," Elisabeth, another lieutenant, chimed in. "This is the work we should be doing."

At her side, Malik, a captain, nodded. "Worth the road-show, for sure."

"Thank you all for holding the fort while I was on the move." She claimed the chair next to Avery. "I've got a few recruitment targets lined up as well. I'll push those through to your tablets as soon as Holt finishes the background checks. Take a look. See if you or any of your soldiers have connections, and if you want to help me with our pitch to them, let me know."

"Is that what Holt's been so busy with?" Connor, on the other side of Avery, asked.

"Unfortunately not." All eyes shot to her. "Which is the last agenda item I need to discuss with you. Some of you have already been brought in on this, but all of you need to be up to speed. You're all aware that Chris's family owns an auto body shop in North Beach?"

"Yeah, the best in the city," Grant, another junior captain, said. "My dad got his vintage 'Vette restored there."

"I want pictures," Helena told him, then addressed the larger group again. "I was at the shop on Friday with Chris's sister, Celia, when there was a drive-by shooting."

"Who was the target?" Connor asked.

"We're working on that determination. Celia's ex-husband was not a good man, and the company he kept was even worse. The drive-by could have been a warning or retribution connected to him." She moved to tap her nails and covered the tick by drumming them on the table instead. "Or to us."

"But aren't we square with everyone?" Alice gestured with her tablet. "This looked like it."

"By all accounts we are, but we can't discount the fact it

might be someone testing our new structure, which means they might test you and your soldiers too. Eyes and ears open and report anything suspicious."

"Copy that," Malik said.

"Okay, that's it. Keep me posted on your ops." As operatives around the table stood, Helena locked eyes with each of her lieutenants. "A minute, please."

Avery, Victoria, Alice, and Elisabeth hung back while the captains filed out and back to their third-floor offices, executive support staff as far as the public and the first and second floor Madigan Cold Storage employees knew.

"You didn't tell them about Ferriello or the Bratva," Victoria said.

"Fuck," Elisabeth cursed, and Alice whistled low. "That's who you think this is?"

"Those are two of the three places where our organization's work and Dex's less than stellar associates intersect," Helena said. "We should know more in the next couple days. Until then, keep an extra close eye on any connections or moves that affect us, particularly as it concerns the Bratva."

"Why didn't you tell the group as a whole?" Alice asked.

"Because if this isn't the Russian mob, I don't want to raise the alarm and purposefully or accidentally start anything with them. No reason to stir shit up, especially from our end. Our contact there has been briefed and she's on standby if we need to escalate matters. Hawes is working the Ferriello angle."

"And the third person?" Elisabeth asked.

"In jail. He may be connected, but obviously, it's unlikely he was the shooter." She stood and her lieutenants with her. "When information solidifies, I'll brief the group again."

"That'll work," Alice said, and Elisabeth nodded too.

There was a knock on the door, and Hawes stuck his head inside the room. "Need you," he said to Helena.

One look and she knew something was wrong. Her heart leapt into her throat, worry for Celia slamming into her. A more acute version of the worry that had kept her up half the night—Was she putting Celia in danger?—the other half the night full of fantasies stoked by the real life one from yesterday—Could she pull away now even if she knew she should?

"Go," Avery said, sensing the urgency too. "We'll make sure the operatives are square."

She caught up with Hawes halfway to the hall of executive offices. "Celia?"

"Fine. At the shop with Chris."

She let out a held breath. "What's going on, then?"

"Oak was trying to reach you. When he couldn't, he called Holt."

"Something's happened?"

"You could say that," Hawes said, grim-faced as they passed his and Chris's offices. They turned into Holt's office, and on one of the monitors of Holt's full command setup, Oak stood under an umbrella, the collar of his long wool trench turned up, outside of San Quentin State Prison.

"Oak," she said. "What's going on?"

He shouted over the pouring rain. "Michael Griffin is dead."

The floor didn't fall out from under her, but it was a near thing. She flailed out a hand for the closest chair back, the one her brother sat in. "What the fuck?"

"Took the words right out of my mouth." Oak sighed, the video call window wobbling. "I came out here to meet with him, like we talked about, and found out he was murdered last night."

"Murdered?" Hawes said.

Oak nodded. "Strangled in his cell."

"Fuck," Helena cursed. "Do they have any idea who?"

"Still investigating," he said. "I did confirm he was here Friday. He wasn't your shooter. But that's all I've got. You're gonna have to get the rest of your answers another way."

"If you learn anything else about what happened there," Hawes said, "let us know."

"Will do." He hung up, and Helena sank into the chair next to Holt. "Two guesses who executed that hit."

"Only need one," Holt said. "The Ferriellos don't have any known associates in there."

"But the Bratva do." She put both elbows on the desk and hung her head in her hands, fingers clutching the roots of her hair. "Fuck! This is us."

Holt gently clasped her shoulder. "We don't know that, Hena. Lenny is in the middle of this, and he's connected to Dex."

"Wait," she said, lifting her head. "Lenny?"

He withdrew his hand and his fingers flew across the keyboard, another screen flickering to life. "Surveillance footage from the storage facility." On it, a generic four-door sedan pulled in front of a garage-sized unit. The passenger door opened and out stepped Lenny. A minute later, Lenny drove out the Charger that had shot up the shop.

"How the fuck do Michael and Lenny know each other?"

"Still digging."

Hawes stepped to the side of the monitor wall and pointed at the car Lenny had stepped out of. "Whose car is that?"

"Adrian Zima's."

"Fucking hell." Helena dropped her arms, crossing them in front of her, at the same time Hawes asked, "What the hell were they up to?"

"Getting someone's attention," Helena said.

"They've got ours," Hawes said, following her train of thought.

"And we need to get the Bratva's before they do."

And in the meantime, she needed to stay as far away from Celia as possible.

SEVENTEEN

Bill drove the Bentley back into the shop yard and his smile was big enough to see through the windshield. He swung the car around behind Celia and pulled next to where she stood, the driver's-side window rolled down. "She rides like a dream."

Celia returned the smile as she wiped her hands on a rag. "*You're* dream, Bill. You deserve it."

"Thanks, Cee."

"You have any issues, just give us a call."

"How about I have some friends give you a call when they need work done?"

"Always happy for the business."

The wrinkles at the corners of his eyes deepened. "I'll be sure to send them your way."

Celia sensed those wrinkles were born of hard times, and she was happy to be the cause of them in better ones. It made keeping the smile on her own face easier. "All right." She slapped the roof of the car. "Get out of here and enjoy your ride."

Once the Bentley cleared the lot, Celia relaxed her cheeks and blew out a long slow breath. She inhaled again, holding it, as she checked her phone.

Her stomach sank. Her **Dinner tonight?** text to Helena remained read but unanswered.

The day-long radio silence was the complete opposite of yesterday evening at the shop and late last night over texts, where their heated back-and-forth had continued. Celia had deleted the messages before going to sleep, not wanting the kids to accidentally find them, or worse yet, Gloria or Chris, but just thinking about them now, about how Helena had directed her every move with the vibrator, made Celia blush.

But since their brief exchange that morning, sweet and in-line with yesterday—Celia's **Weird waking up here again** and Helena's **You're always welcome in my house... and my bed**—there'd been no responses to Celia's other texts. All of them read and unanswered.

A flirtatious midday check-in, a selfie taken on the dolly where they'd gotten frisky yesterday.

A picture of the finished Bentley.

The dinner ask.

Had Celia pushed too hard? Maybe the flirty picture had been too much. But after yesterday evening, after last night, after Helena's first and only text this morning...

Behind her, Lorenzo cleared his throat. "You're glaring at that phone like you want it to explode."

With messages would be good. Instead, it and the woman she wanted to hear from remained silent. She tucked the phone away and walked back into the bay where Zo was working on an after-market mod of a Urus.

Less weight, more power, and a big paycheck for the shop. "Was just hoping to hear from someone."

"Miss Madigan?"

She ran her hand along the custom spoiler and ducked her chin, hiding the blush that automatically came from being called out on her crush by the man who was her late father's best friend.

At the front end of the car, Lorenzo lowered the hood. "I'm just glad you two are okay after Friday."

Okay was a relative term, but to her staff, she wanted to project calm and normalcy. She'd filled them in yesterday morning on the previous week's events. She'd had to in order to explain the leftover forensic dust, bullet holes, boarded-up windows, and spray paint, the new windshield that had been rush-ordered for the Bentley, and the new surveillance and extra muscle around the shop. Grant, it had turned out, was a bit of a garage rat himself, his grandfather a mechanic for a trucking company, his dad a vintage car enthusiast, so he knew how to make himself useful when needed and how to get out of the way when he wasn't. Or maybe that was just him doing his job, no doubt one of the best at it if he worked for the Madigans.

"I feel bad I left when I did," Lorenzo said.

"Don't, Zo." She crossed to his end of the car. "I'm glad you were out of here and safe, and thank you for the extra work on the Bentley."

"Was a pleasure, and I'm sure Miss Madigan is just busy. She always seems that way."

Not untrue, but Celia didn't think that was the entire reason for the freeze out. "You got it in here?" she asked. "I need to do some paperwork in the office."

"You go on. I've got it." He used his rag to wipe a

smudge off the Lambo's hood. "Gonna finish up a few things, then I'll clean up and close up."

"Thanks."

She tossed her own rag in the hamper, washed her hands and forearms at the sink, then headed to the office, Zo's words continuing to rattle around in her head. Maybe she was overreacting. Yes, Helena had disappeared on her for months, but she'd promised that wouldn't happen again. That she would stay this time, and she'd kept that promise through the chaos of the past weekend. If Helena was too busy to respond to texts, it was probably because of Celia, because Helena was out there doing everything possible to make sure she and her family were safe. She sat behind her desk and tapped out a new message on her phone. **Let me know if you need anything.**

When no reply text or bubbles appeared after a minute, she set the phone aside, facedown, and focused on the parts order that had to get submitted by end of day. Fifteen minutes later, her phone vibrated. She snatched it off the desk, flipped it over, and grinned at the text alert from Helena. She opened the message.

I'm good. Let Chris or Grant know if there are any issues tonight.

Her smile died. Helena's words were cold and efficient, like a work text or email. A brush-off. Granted, it was easy to misread emotion, or the absence of it, over texts, but this message was clear, especially after the day long silence. She wouldn't be hearing from or seeing Helena again tonight. She slumped in her chair, gaze drifting to the couch where twenty-four hours ago Helena, in blue satin, had been spread across her thighs, riding her hand and biting her shoulder as the two of them shared what Celia had thought was an amazing experience.

Had she dreamed it all?

She blinked fast, trying to hold back threatening tears. Was she making excuses for Helena, same as she'd done for Dex all those years? During all his absences? She angrily wiped away the tears that defied her. She fucking knew better. She and Helena had barely struck up a friendship again. Why had she thought this time would be any different? Why had she let her heart and body hope for more?

The desk phone rang, and she set aside her cell to answer it. "Perri—" Voice rough, she cleared her throat and started again. "Perri Auto Works."

An electronic voice talked over her. "San Francisco County Jail," it said. "Call for Celia Perri from Dexter Russo. Do you accept?"

She opened her mouth to say no, then caught the refusal on the tip of her tongue. She didn't want to talk to Dex, but maybe if she did, he'd be stupid enough to say something they could use to catch the drive-by shooter.

"Yes."

Two clicks later, Dex greeted her with a surprised, "You took my call."

"Obviously."

"I'm sorry," he said. "I started that wrong." She was sure he wore an artificial smile to match the artificial sweetness in his voice, fake sugar that had kept her hanging on for far too long. "How are you, Cee?"

She kept her own voice as flat as possible, steeling herself and not giving him an ounce of her emotional capital that was already running low. "Fine."

"I'd hoped to see you at the station or here at the jail. Thought maybe you'd bring the kids by to see me."

"In jail?"

"I'm their father."

"Maybe you should have thought about that before breaking into the place that provides for their food and clothes."

Sugar quickly turned to venom. "You sent your brother and that other lawyer after me instead."

"I did."

"They're dangerous, Celia."

"Because they helped protect me from you?"

Turned to cajoling. "You don't need protection from me."

She covered the *bullshit* she wanted to utter with the unvarnished truth. "You hit me, Dexter, and for years before that you abused me in other ways. I'm done with it."

"I didn't abuse you. I would never do that."

"You don't know the meaning of the word, Dex, and I won't expose my children to that kind of toxic environment any longer."

"*Our* children."

The swing from sugar to venom to sugar was like being on an amusement park ride. Observing it from the ground now, instead of being on the ride itself, she was so fucking glad to be off it. "That's the one good thing you did, Dex. You gave me those kids, but beyond that, not much other good came out of our marriage."

"I gave you a life," he spat.

"Bullshit." She let some of her fury and conviction loose. Yes, it was expended capital, but for the longer gain. "*I* made a life for *my* family." She wanted him to hear how pissed she was, wanted him to know she was confident enough in herself to kick him to the curb for good. She could support her family and live her life without him. "You're not a part of that anymore. We're moving on. *I'm* moving on."

"Moving on? With who?" For once in his life, Dex put two and two together. "With that lawyer bitch? The way she treated me was—"

"Her name is Helena, and I'm sure you deserved whatever she did to you. I only wish I'd had the chance."

"Celia, you don't—"

"Goodbye, Dex."

"What about the arraignment?" he blurted out. "Will you be there tomorrow?"

"No, but I'll be sure to have Helena give you my regards."

She hung up before he could respond, almost missing the receiver cradle because her hands were shaking so badly. Fight or flight—she recognized the response now—and for the first time in her life, she'd fought back against Dex. She was proud of herself, but she was also shaken, expecting reprisal even if she knew it wouldn't be coming. She needed to talk to someone.

She grabbed her cell, thumb hovering over the speed dial for Helena, until the earlier pain and doubt flooded back in. Already weakened, it would have taken out her knees if she weren't sitting. As it was, it tossed and turned her insides, leaving her even more of a mess, which Helena no longer wanted to have anything to do with, no matter what she'd led Dex to believe. She scrolled down her contacts list to the counselor and survivor who led her domestic violence support group.

"Celia, hey," Bonnie answered. "How's it going?"

"It's been a rough few days," Celia said. "And I just had a bit of a run in with my ex."

"Are you okay?"

"Yes, it was a phone call, and I actually stood up to him, but now I can't stop shaking. I could use someone to talk to."

"Good for you, and after that kind of a rush, the crash is totally normal," Bonnie said. "Caffe Trieste in a half hour?"

Celia sighed a deep, relieved breath, her first one all day. "I'll see you soon."

EIGHTEEN

Helena slid in beside the man dressed in worn jeans and a long-sleeve tee and rested her forearms on the metal rail overlooking the lush green canopy of Cal Academy's indoor rainforest. "Do you come here every week because you actually like science and nature?"

Hawes assumed the same position on the other side of August Ferriello. "Or is it because there's a mark within five feet at all times?"

Maybe even closer in here. The rainforest walkways were narrow and the flow of foot traffic steady. Two steps back and she'd be right in the stream of it. And then there was outside the giant glass dome where the multi-floor California Academy of Sciences teemed with countless visitors and patrons.

"Does it look like I'm scoping marks?" August replied, his voice rougher than she recalled, and Helena wondered when he'd last spoken to anyone. She didn't wonder, though, what August's sharp eyes were assessing.

"Marks, no," Helena said. "Exits, yes."

He aimed his smirking light brown eyes at her. "You always were the smart one."

"Yet you slept with the other one?"

"Mistakes were made." August resumed his roving downward stare and jutted his chin toward the crowd below. "Not like I'd steal from any of them."

"You gone clean?"

"Ninety-nine percent of tourists aren't worth it."

"That's right," Hawes said. "You'd rather rip off us locals instead."

August pushed off the rail, only to turn and rest back against it, arms crossed over his broad chest. "I hear congratulations are in order."

Hawes leaned a hip next to his and adjusted the cuffs of his sleeves beneath his suit coat. "It'd be nice to have my father's cufflinks for the wedding."

August shrugged. "I have no idea what you're talking about."

"Oh?" Hawes said, a whip in his tone that made Helena worry for August's safety. "So that wasn't you who fucked me, then stole the family jewels while I slept?"

Chris's growl through the comm in Helena's ear was likewise worrisome, but at the same time highly amusing. In what was turning out to be a brutal day, made more so by the distance she was forcing herself to keep from the one person she wanted to get closer to, she welcomed the momentary amusing distraction of Hawes snipping at his one-night stand while Chris fumed.

"I don't think that ex-fed would be marrying you if I'd stolen *all* the jewels."

"Get to the fucking point," Chris ordered.

He and August were apparently on the same page, the

latter returning his attention to Helena. "What do you want?"

"Need you to get a message to Francis," she said.

August's blank face was the picture of indifference. "I haven't spoken to my brother in years. I want nothing to do with him or the rest of them."

Helena believed that, to a point. She wagered the present situation was beyond said point. "His drug dealer"—the disinterested mask cracked, his eyes narrowing—"is tight with a Bratva soldier"—and shattered, his eyes widening. She'd wagered correctly.

"Your family," Hawes said, "doesn't want to fuck with the Bratva any more than ours does."

"With Frankie, who the fuck knows." He scrubbed his hands over his face, then let his arms fall to his sides. "He'd be stupid enough to try, especially if he's on something."

"Cocaine," Hawes confirmed. "It's possible his dealer—a guy named Lenny—doesn't even know his other buddy is Bratva."

"Lenny's not the sharpest tool in the shed," Helena explained. "It's likely he's trying to impress your brother while his coconspirator is trying to impress his Bratva bosses."

On heightened alert, August's gaze swept their surroundings again. Helena wasn't worried. Holt or Chris or the other operatives on-site would tell them if they were being watched or followed.

"It's still not good," August said, lowering his volume. Helena wasn't worried about that either. Their voices wouldn't carry past the comms over the steady drum of trudging feet and the ambient rainforest sounds. That's why she and Hawes had waited to approach him there.

"Didn't you just negotiate a ceasefire with Frank? Why can't you go talk to him?"

"Because we trust him even less than we trust you," Helena replied. "He could be working with the Bratva too for all we know."

August braced his hands behind him, knuckles white where they curled around the rail, and let his head hang back on a frustrated groan. "Fuck, I hope not."

The plight of the older, responsible brother. Helena felt a tinge of regret for being so hard on both of hers.

"Or he could be flying off the handle and mounting a challenge against the Bratva," Hawes said, the oldest brother calculating the worst possible outcome.

August righted his head on a glare. "These scenarios aren't getting any better."

Helena patted his scruffy cheek. "You always were the smart one."

"We can't be the ones to set it off," Hawes said. "But we need to know your brother's organization isn't involved."

"Or," Helena said, "you could just steal the bad guy?"

One corner of his mouth twitched, fighting a sly smile. "Isn't that your specialty?"

Hawes chuckled from his other side and pushed off the rail. "You're not as out of touch as you pretend to be, Augustus."

Helena laughed out loud. She'd been waiting for Hawes to deliver that bullet the entire conversation, knowing he wouldn't be able to resist pulling the trigger, knowing he needed that shot of revenge. He'd hit the bull's-eye, August's face the picture of fury. Hawes skedaddled out of his reach, into the moving current of people, and Helena darted between them, just in case August tried to give chase. None of them needed an incident in public, even if it did look like a jilted lover's squabble. "We'll let you get back to your work," she said, then fired a shot of her own. "I hope whoever it is contracting you for artifacts is paying you enough for all your time here."

He let the anger go as quickly as it had come, relaxing back against the rail, and his gaze took on an attractive fondness as he swept it around the museum again. "I don't mind it."

"Didn't think you did," she said with a wink, then disappeared into the sea of people with her brother, leaving the thief to his work.

NINETEEN

"If I didn't know better," Avery said, "I'd think you were more interested in your phone than these proceedings."

Helena lifted her gaze and surveyed the courtroom, counting counsel and defendants. The crowd had thinned out considerably since they'd first entered and claimed their spots on the last gallery bench, but Dex was last on the arraignment docket, and by her count, there were still five other defendants to go.

"You'd think right." She returned to scrolling through her texts with Celia. The message she'd sent yesterday afternoon had had its intended effect. Not another peep from Celia, and Helena had never been more miserable. Not the recent winter months she'd gone without seeing her. Not the summer and fall before then that she'd spent watching and wanting from across the garage bay. Not the sharp pang of desire she'd felt when she'd first laid eyes on Celia Perri.

Monday night had been the single best sexual experience of her life, and she'd had her fair share, with men and women. But none of those had ever been as satisfying—or as emotional. She'd liked most of her past sexual partners, but that was as far as her connection to them had gone. As far as she'd allowed it to go. Until Celia. Celia had gotten under her skin, knocked down her walls, and now that Helena knew how good it could be, everything else— everyone else—paled in comparison. And yet, how could she put her own pleasure, her own happiness above Celia's life? Above the life and livelihood of Gloria and the kids? There was the real push.

"Just text her back," Avery said.

"And tell her what?" Helena snapped. "Her family's life's work was shot up, and she could have been killed because someone is after my family in order to curry favor with the Russian mob."

"We don't know that." Avery tilted her head toward where Dex sat in the front row with the other defendants waiting their turn. "Maybe it was a message for that asshole."

"You think he's worth all this hassle?"

Avery shrugged. "It's a lot of debt, and he's a known flight risk."

True, but Helena still didn't see it. A borrowed car, jacked with custom parts, then abandoned. Because of Dex? "August said it wasn't his brother. So it's Lenny gone rogue, Lenny gone stupid, or Lenny working with Zima to climb the Bratva ladder." She recalled what August had said yesterday. "These scenarios aren't getting any better."

Avery shifted on the bench, crossing a leg toward her and stretching an arm out on the bench behind her, giving up any pretense she was paying attention either. "And this prevents you from pursuing something with Celia how?

And don't pretend like you don't want to." She lowered her voice and leaned closer. "If you don't, you're fucking blind, because one, she's hot as fuck, and two, she's good people."

"Which is why I need to steer clear. I've got nothing to offer her."

"That's utter horse shit." So much for keeping her volume low and so much for courtroom manners. Avery flipped off the few people left in the gallery who'd turned to glare their direction. They turned back to the proceedings, and Avery turned back to her, her dark gaze resolute. "You are smart, dedicated, and gorgeous."

"I'm dangerous."

"Stop making excuses. You always do this, come up with some reason to push people away. Your brothers won't call you out on it, but I'm tired of watching you be alone. You get to be happy too."

"I can't expose—"

"Boss, can you honestly say she's in any more danger from you than from Chris or any of us or from her ex or any of those other criminals he's sitting up there with?"

Helena hung her head, chuckling softly.

"I was in danger too." The drastic shift in Avery's tone made Helena glance up again, only to find Avery's gaze fixed on a spot over Helena's shoulder, on a time in the past. "Amelia found me, got me out of that, and fuck, boss" —she refocused on Helena and on the present—"so far, besides your grandmother, Amelia's been the most dangerous one of you. But if not for her, I have no doubt I'd be dead. I wouldn't be here today, monitoring this asshole's arraignment because, oh, let me think, we're trying to keep his ex-wife *safe*."

Helena rested her head against her friend and colleague's shoulder. "I'm glad you're here."

"You're good people too." Avery patted her knee. "Even if I do have to knock some sense into each of you sometimes."

"I just want to do right by her," Helena said. "She was raising a kid when I was still acting like one. She shouldn't have to worry—"

"She's a mom. She's wired that way, whether it's about herself, her kids, her family, or you. I know you're used to losing people—your parents, your grandparents, Holt for a time, Amelia—but that woman, she'll stick if you let her. And besides, is it your decision to make? Shouldn't she be the one to decide how much risk she can handle?"

As the last few defendants before Dex were processed through, Helena turned Avery's words over in her head. And as Dex finally stood and the judge read off the charges, reviewed his rap sheet, and recounted his many, many absences, correctly determining he was a flight risk and denying his request for reduced bail, a lump formed in Helena's throat and a knot settled in her stomach. The way she'd been treating Celia wasn't all that different from the way Dex used to. Taking away her choices. Keeping her on the outside. Keeping her in the dark.

She understood now why Celia had met with her support group counselor last night, and it made Helena sick to her stomach to think she'd put Celia into one of the very situations she was trying to protect her from. As for the other, Avery was right. Celia was strong, the strongest woman Helena knew. If she wasn't afraid, if she was willing to take a risk on her, then Helena had to stop being afraid to do the same.

Avery bumped her arm. "And that's a wrap."

The gavel fell, and Helena pried herself out of her own head. They shuffled into the aisle, shaking hands with the departing public defender. At the front of the room, the judge and clerk exited one direction, and the bailiff led Dex the other way toward the prisoners' entrance. At the door, Dex glanced over his shoulder and spied her and Avery. "This is your fault," he sneered.

"Nope," Helena said. "Pretty sure all the evidence points to you."

"Because you planted it."

"Not this time," she said with a wink.

The bailiff dragged a fuming Dexter the rest of the way out of the courtroom, and Helena and Avery headed toward the gallery doors. Helena's hand was on the handle when the unmistakable *pop* of a gunshot blasted from somewhere behind them.

Helena didn't have to give the order; she and Avery worked together as seamlessly as she worked with her brothers. They broke to opposite sides of the courtroom, crouching behind the last row of benches. She peeked over the bench. No one but them in the courtroom, confirming the gunfire had come from the hallway Dex had been led into.

"Clear," she said. "Shots in the hallway." She and Avery had maybe five seconds before the guards charging the opposite direction, from the foyer, barged in. "Go!"

They sprinted up either side of the courtroom, Helena grabbing weapons as she streaked across the front of the familiar space. Pens, wires, the bailiff's Bible. Avery opened the door for her, and she ran through, two pens and the Bible at the ready. Not as good as her knives, but she could make do. Assuming she could get a lock on her target. Unfortunately, the elevator doors closed on Zima and a still-cuffed Dexter before she could strike. Zima, though, already had. The bailiff was slumped against the wall, blood oozing from a gunshot wound to his right shoulder. Helena dropped the Bible, stripped off the scarf hanging loosely around her neck, and flung it at Avery. "Apply pressure. Catch up."

Avery caught the scarf and dropped to her knees next to the bailiff, fast at work. "Copy."

Helena ran flat out for the stairwell door, flashing her access badge. She skipped down the stairs, landing and bounding off every third one, riding the momentum. She reached the ground floor only a few seconds behind Zima and Dex, who were hustling toward a utility van, Lenny standing at the open back doors.

She opened her mouth to call after them but then an arm circled her waist and a hand covered her mouth. "What do you think you're doing?" Avery whispered from behind her.

Their height difference gave Avery a few-second advantage, enough to haul Helena behind a parked SUV, but once they were out of sight, Helena bit the inside of her palm, rammed the insole of Avery's foot, and wrenched herself free. Spinning, she traded three quick jabs with Avery, then finally got her calf hooked behind the taller woman's and her forearm braced across her chest, shoving Avery against the side of the SUV. "Nice moves, but you have to let me do this."

"Which is what?"

"Giving them what they want."

"They've got what they want. Dex."

And Zima was going to make off with him if she didn't end this standoff quickly. But she had to make sure Avery took the right message back to her family. "Until they call and try to ransom him. Until Celia finds out and has to worry even more about her kids' deadbeat dad. They don't really want Dex. They want me. The queen."

Avery smiled. "And you think you're not good enough for her."

Trusting she'd won the argument, and hearing another one escalating between Zima and Lenny, Helena released Avery and dug her phone out of her pocket. "You get the plates on the van?"

Avery, always on the lookout, always acutely aware of their surroundings, rattled off the numbers and letters.

"Good." Helena handed over her phone. While Holt could track it to find her, so could any number of other parties who might try a third-party rip-off. And no telling what Zima or the Bratva would do with that phone if they got their hands on it. "Rally the troops. Come get me."

"You could just take him out."

"Or I could make sure this only goes as high as Zima and make sure no one else makes this kind of play against us."

"Copy." Avery made an *oof* sound and pretended to fall to the ground, the noise interrupting Zima and Lenny's argument.

Hands raised, Helena stepped around the hood of the SUV. "It's me you want, isn't it, Adrian? That's why you shot up the shop."

"What's going on?" Dex said from where he lay sideways in the back of the van.

"Yeah, Adrian, what the hell?" Lenny added. "I thought

we were just gonna intimidate Dex again. Like with the drive-by. Convince him to give us the money he owes—"

Zima popped Lenny in the temple with his elbow, a swift hard blow. The dealer folded like a rag doll, right into the back of the truck, unconscious.

"Get in," Zima said to her.

She pointed at Lenny and Dex. "Let those two go. Bratva's not gonna care about a drug dealer and a petty criminal."

"I think I'll keep them. May ditch the one," Zima said, a flick of his eyes toward Lenny before he pointed the gun at Dex, who squirmed farther back in the van like a fucking idiot. "He's my insurance that you cooperate. If you're willing to trade yourself for him, what else will you do?"

Oh, if he only knew. She'd save that surprise for later when she had all the intel she needed. She climbed into the van, and Zima slammed the doors shut, plunging them into darkness.

Until the fucking idiot among them let her know exactly where he was. "What the hell?" Dex whined. "This is all Celia's fault. I told her you were bad—"

She punched him square in the mouth, silencing him so she could think about how to make her next move against Zima and about the move after that—how to win Celia back.

TWENTY

What was it Celia had said? *If she never had to be back inside the police station again it would be too soon.* Well, three days later was way too fucking soon.

"Anything else about the phone call from Dex you can tell me?" Brax asked.

She shook her head. "No, that was everything." She bit her lip, afraid to give words to the fear that had been gnawing inside her since Grant had spirited her out of the shop two hours ago. But she was more afraid not to have an answer. "Is this because of me? Because of what I said to Dex? Did I do this?"

Brax stood, circled his desk, and claimed the visitor chair next to her. Three days and another incident had not done the chief any favors. He looked even more flattened, more exhausted than he had on Sunday, but there was still something about him that calmed her, that made her believe he'd help make everything all right. "By all accounts, Dex had no idea what was going on. No matter what you said to him on that call, this would have likely still happened. This was not your fault." He held her fidgeting hands in both of his. "It's hard loving them," he said, and the same pain that had haunted Holt's face the past week emerged on Brax's. He wasn't talking about Dex or exes anymore. He was talking about the other people— the Madigans—who played a starring role in both their lives. His Adam's apple bobbed, and he licked his lips like he was searching for the right words to make her feel better. She appreciated that he gave her the truth instead. "I'm not gonna lie," he said. "This will probably not be the last time we meet like this, but they always manage to pull through. We just have to have faith and do what we can to help."

"And pick up the pieces after?"

"Someone has to." He smiled, a weak yet fond thing. "I'm always here, Cee, if you need me."

She reversed her grip, squeezing his fingers, sensing Brax needed the comfort, the ally, as much as she did. "Thank you, Chief."

The door behind them opened, Chris poking in his head. "We need to get back to the house," he said. "You good?"

"We're good here." Brax released her hands and stood, offering her a hand up then circling back behind his desk. "Everyone else safe there?" he asked Chris, and while Celia knew he was asking generally, there were two people she thought he wanted to know about in particular.

Chris nodded. "Everyone else is locked down at the mansion. We'll keep you posted. Do the same?"

"Of course."

They slipped out of his office and out a back exit. "Mom and the kids?" she asked as they hustled down the stairs.

"Also at the house."

"Good." She waited until they were out of the parking garage, she with Chris in Hawes's borrowed Benz, Grant and Malik trailing behind them in her SUV, before she asked another of the questions that had been nagging her. "How did she get taken? Wasn't Avery with her?"

"Avery tried to stop her, but there's only one person who can best Helena in hand-to-hand combat, and in this case, I'm not sure even Mel would've won." He handed her his phone, a video ready to play. "She was determined."

By the time Celia finished the video, she was equal parts awed and furious. "She gave herself up?"

"To protect Dex and to find out exactly what is going on."

"She mentioned the Bratva. As in the Russian mob Bratva?"

At a stoplight, Chris took his phone back and dropped it in the cup holder. "You can't—"

Anger won out. "Fuck it, Christopher, just tell me what you can." The full name got his attention, as did her tone no doubt. It was the same one their mother used whenever they got up to something they shouldn't. When he continued to hesitate, she wound it up more. "I know there are limits, need to know and all that bullshit, but the woman I—"

His face whipped her direction, brow arched.

Fuck it. Helena had traded herself to keep her worthless ex safe. No doubt to keep *her* safe and to keep *her* from having to deal with the fallout. The least Celia could do was admit the truth. "My *friend*, who I would like to be more, just surrendered herself to the person who shot up the shop."

Once across King Street, Chris sped up, cutting down

side streets and up those less crowded than Third, swiftly making his way through SOMA. "Dex and Lenny are idiots," he said. "They got tangled up with a guy who is low level Russian mob and didn't even know it."

"The blond one?"

"Adrian Zima. He's trying to make a name for himself. Climb the ranks."

"By going after the Madigans?"

Chris nodded, and Celia propped her elbow on the window, forehead in the palm of her hand, all the pieces finally coming together. "That's why Helena's been pushing me away."

"She was trying to protect you, Cee."

Fuck, that was all she'd ever been trying to do.

"She has a hard time turning it off," Chris continued. "Last year, she was the bait on one of our ops, and we had to talk her out of doing it again on another after she became the head of the organization."

Celia swung her gaze to Chris. "I thought that was Hawes."

"Not since last summer, and she feels more responsibility than ever. For everyone. Operatives, family, *friends* she might also like to be more."

And now she'd gone and put her life on the line, playing the bait again, to protect Celia and her family. From the Russian mob. "Are the Bratva enemies?"

Chris impatiently drummed his thumbs on the steering wheel as they waited at another stoplight. "Relations are actually better than ever, but this situation is unpredictable."

That sounded ominous. "Meaning it might not matter?"

"Hawes and Helena were supposed to meet with the Bratva tonight." The light turned green, they turned onto Geary, and Chris gunned the Benz, home free for at least a few blocks on the cross-town expressway. "We were hoping to head this off."

"But now one of their people have her. The head of a rival organization." And there she went, making it sound even more ominous. It wasn't so much a hummingbird in her stomach now as a raven doing barrel rolls.

"We can't rival the Bratva," Chris said, "but we can cause them trouble, unless we convince them Zima is more trouble."

Go with the giant black bird, then. She didn't see how she had another option. Hold on tight, use everything Helena had taught her, summon up all the borrowed and earned confidence, and go save the woman she would like to have more with too. "All right, then, what the fuck are we waiting for?"

Chris pulled into the Madigans' driveway and shifted in his seat, angling toward her, and Celia had no idea his eyebrow could climb that high. "We?"

"She's in this because of me." Celia pointed at herself, then at him, then at the house where the rest of her family had been sheltered the past week. "Because of *our* family. And because Dex is a fucking idiot who led them right to something—someone—they could leverage. That's what you all call it, yes?"

His brow lowered as one corner of his mouth rose. "You hear more than you let on."

"Dex would never do what Helena did for me today, and I'll be damned if I let that asshole be the reason something happens to her." She unfastened her seatbelt and flung it off, hand on the door, hand on the next step of her life, and she was ready to pull the handle. Ready to open the door to the chaos and love that could come with it. "I'm not sitting this one out."

TWENTY-ONE

Celia was over thirty, and tonight was the first time she'd stepped inside a club. That's what happened when you had your first kid in high school. She'd never had nights out at the club with friends, never had a wild spring break with college roommates, never danced to thumping music and flashing lights with a would-be partner. Looking down from the mezzanine balcony of Club Sterling, she wasn't too sure she cared about the club part of what she'd missed. The loud music made her head hurt, the strobe lights didn't help, and the dance floor below was way too packed for her to ever feel comfortable there.

"How did this place become neutral ground?" she asked Hawes, who rested against the balcony rail beside her.

They'd read her in back at the house, explaining the basics of the meet—the location, the parties, the objectives.

"How much do you want to know?" he said.

She waved him off. "Forget I asked." She was here for Helena, and she would be again in the future for Helena and any of her family—Perris and Madigans—when they needed her, but as seldom as possible in this direct a role. Mia was spot on the other night when describing her place in all this. Five minutes inside Club Sterling, five hours of the fucking raven doing barrel rolls in her stomach, and Celia agreed one hundred percent with her daughter. "When this is all over, I just want to be the partner who is the mom-friend of the family and who makes sure all of you are bandaged and fed. The rest of what you do..." She closed her eyes and covered her ears.

Hawes gently tugged down her hands. "Her partner?"

"Yeah, if I can get through that hard head of hers."

Chuckling, Hawes dropped a peck on the top of her head. "Helena needs you. We all do. I think back on my parents, on my grandparents, and they never had anyone on the outside to ground them. They got lost in this world, and it cost them their lives and freedom." Celia was so surprised by the regret, the vulnerability, the warmth in his voice, that she reached out to clasp his hand. He squeezed back, more firmly, more genuinely than she expected. "We're trying to do things differently. Better. *You* help make us better."

If she could do that for the Madigans, it made her feel a little less guilty for all the trouble they'd gone through this week to keep her and her family safe. "Thank you."

The moment was interrupted by a click in her ear, startling her at first until she remembered the comm device there.

"What is it?" Hawes said, and it was equally startling to hear him next to her and directly in her ear.

"Patching Oak through," Holt said. Another couple clicks, then Holt reported, "Oak, we're all on."

The lawyer? Celia mouthed to Hawes, who nodded.

Made sense as Helena had mentioned a meeting with him on Monday.

"Two updates," Oak said. "It was a Bratva soldier that murdered Griffin. The soldier hung himself in his cell this morning."

"Fuck," Hawes cursed. "The other piece?"

"The connection between Griffin and Lenny. Griffin's ex-wife is tight with Lenny's sister. Lenny told his sister he needed some wheels, and the ex mentioned the car sitting in a storage unit she's justifiably bitter about paying for."

"So Lenny helped himself to the car."

"Looks like it." The ambient noise in the background grew louder, Oak entering a restaurant, judging by the clink of silverware and a hostess asking for his party name. He begged her pardon for a minute, then asked them, "You need anything else from me? My husband might murder you himself if I continue to keep him waiting for our anniversary dinner."

"We're set, thanks," Hawes said. "Have a good dinner, and happy anniversary."

Oak clicked off with a "Thanks," and once Holt confirmed "Clear," Hawes added, "Find out where they're dining and pay for the meal. Send over some champagne too."

"Already done," Holt said.

Celia ducked her chin and smiled, happy her brother had found a good man and a good family to attach to their own. All the good it had led to.

"Remy entering," Connor reported.

"Details on the women?" Hawes said to Holt, back to business.

"Pulling information now," Holt replied. "I'll compile and send through the server. On your device in five."

"Remy, nine o'clock," Victoria said, just as motion at the far end of the mezzanine, on the other side of Hawes, drew Celia's attention.

The crowd parted for a tall, striking woman who strode their direction with as much confidence as Helena typically moved but without the same grace. Remy, on first impression, seemed more the blunt-weapon sort, disguised as she was in skin-tight jeans, knee-high leather boots, and a shimmering metallic top under a leather jacket.

Following Celia's gaze, Hawes rotated, caught sight of Remy and told Holt, "Gotta go." He pocketed his phone as Remy sidled up next to him, front pressed against his side, hand on his shoulder. "You're a new face," she said, blatantly checking out Celia.

Celia projected all the confidence she could muster. Not enough to go toe to toe with this woman, but maybe enough to back her off a step. "I'm the one who took her off the market."

A slow sly smile spread across Remy's face. "Your fiancé's sister?" she asked Hawes.

"The resemblance?"

"The cockiness." Her gaze returned to Celia. "Though I like it much better on you."

"Time's tight, Remy," Hawes said, and the other woman sighed dramatically.

She stepped from Hawes's side to Celia's and hooked an elbow through hers. "I don't know if you know this," she said, starting them walking toward the other end of the mezzanine. "But your brother and his pet mobster are real party poopers."

"Sometime when Helena hasn't been kidnapped," Celia said, keeping Remy talking and friendly as she remained aware of her surroundings. They were in a hallway off the mezzanine, what appeared to be the club's executive offices. "I'll tell you about the old Chris. He wasn't always a party pooper."

Remy howled with laughter, and out of the corner of her eye, Celia caught Hawes's approving smile. Smiles and laughter died, though, as they entered one of the offices to find Lenny gagged and bound to a chair. Across from Lenny, standing behind the desk, was an older man with salt-and-pepper hair and dark blue eyes. Much like the Madigans, had Celia seen him on the street or in a restaurant, she would have assumed he was any other wealthy San Franciscan, not the head of the Russian mob here in Fog City.

Hawes approached the desk, his hand extended. "Dimitri."

"Hawes," Dimitri Petrov greeted, his voice lightly accented. "It's been too long. I've been wanting to tell you I commend what you and your siblings have done with your organization. Made all our lives easier."

"Thank you." He eyed Lenny. "And you brought us a present?"

Lenny squirmed in his chair as if he could sense the combined danger of the three other people in the room. His eyes kept darting back to Celia, beseeching, like he thought she could do anything to get him out of this pickle. "Don't look at me." She motioned around the room. "We're all here because of your poor life choices."

"She's smart too," Remy said with a wink.

"We didn't pick him up," Dimitri answered Hawes's

question. "Someone left him on our doorstep with these." He opened his fist and in his palm were a pair of cufflinks the exact ice-blue shade as Hawes's and Helena's eyes.

He dropped them into Hawes's hand, and Hawes smiled, a cold satisfied thing. "Did you know him?" Hawes asked as he pocketed the jewelry. "Before tonight?"

"He is an associate of Adrian's. Not ours. And I did not nor do I intend to order a hit on your sister."

"But one of your soldiers was involved in one," Hawes said. "And that soldier has her now."

"Not one of mine any longer. He used one of my men in prison to kill someone without authorization. Now I've lost that man. And when I wouldn't take his meet, he went to the Ferriellos. Tried to bargain with them."

"That's how they got him?" Hawes said, approaching Lenny.

"I assume so."

"Did he tell you anything helpful? Like where Zima might be holding my sister?"

Dimitri buttoned his coat as he circled the desk. "Leaving that for you."

"Are you willing to help us?" Hawes's tone was dead even, not letting on which answer he wanted, whether he cared one way or the other. If it were up to Celia, she'd take all the help she could get, but there was way more at play here than she knew or cared to know.

Dimitri came to a stop in front of Hawes. "I won't interfere, and you'll have Remy's assistance."

"And we won't be seen as attacking you through your former soldier."

Dimitri extended a hand. "A truce."

Hawes shook his hand. "A reservation."

The older man smiled, not hiding his fondness. "Call it what you will." He drew back his hand and bowed politely as he passed Celia. "Ms. Perri." He exchanged a few hushed words with Remy by the door, then exited, Remy closing the door behind him.

Hawes had already moved to his next target, roughly pulling down the gag from Lenny's mouth.

"I'm sorry." Lenny coughed, his pleading eyes darting all around, then back to her. "Cee, I'm sorry, I didn't—"

Hawes grabbed his chin and wrenched his face back to him. "You don't get to talk to her." His tone was no longer even. It was cold, hard, all the iciness Celia could never put her finger on crystalized into a sharp, deadly dagger. "Not after the shit you pulled."

"Who are you?" Lenny stuttered.

"You're as clueless as Dex, aren't you?"

"This is his fault." Lenny squirmed in his chair, in Hawes's hold, trying and failing to free himself. "He told me the shop would be empty that time a day."

"*You* thought you were shooting up an empty shop?" Celia said.

"Yes! Dex owed me and Frank money. Adrian said he wanted to get in good with Frank, and so did I. He said this would be a good way to do it. I didn't know he was Russian mob. I swear."

"Now you've got a bigger problem," Hawes said.

Lenny's voice shook as he whispered, "Who are you?"

Bending, Hawes got right in Lenny's face. "They call me the Prince of Killers."

Celia dug her teeth into her bottom lip, holding back her gasp. She reminded herself of the kindness Hawes had shown her outside on the mezzanine, over the past week, over the past six months. Reminded herself of all the good he'd brought to her brother's life, how he'd brought Chris home to them. Told herself he was not only the icy killer he displayed for Lenny.

"And you could have gotten my sister-in-law and my sister killed. You still might." He lifted a hand, right at the level of his hairline. "So that puts you near the top of my shit list. That's not a good place to be, Lenny."

The stench of urine tainted the air and a stain spread across the crotch and down the leg of Lenny's cargo pants.

Hawes didn't flinch. Didn't give up a single intimidating inch. "You're going to tell me what I need to know, starting with a list of everywhere you and Adrian have been together recently."

"And with Dex," Celia nodded.

"And with Dex," Hawes amended, and when Lenny tried again to shirk back, stuttering and protesting, Hawes roared in his face. "Now, Lenny!"

Celia wouldn't have been surprised if Lenny shit his pants right then too. But at least he began to spit out the list of places among his snotting and crying. Over the comm, Holt repeated back each location, followed by rapid-fire typing.

"That's it," Lenny said after he'd given them a half dozen locations. "That's all I know." He tried and failed to wipe his nose on his shoulder, unable to shake loose Hawes's hold. "Do I get to go now?"

"Brax in five," Holt said.

Celia bit her lip again, this time in amusement, at Lenny getting his due, fucking finally, and because she was that damn impressed with her extended family. Hawes hadn't had to tell Holt what to do next. The three of them, four counting Chris, read each other's moves so seamlessly. On Friday it had made her head spin; now it was a comfort, a security blanket against the chill that was obviously the other side of their business.

Hawes released Lenny, straightened, and stepped back. "'Fraid not Lenny. The chief of police will be here to arrest you shortly."

"But I cooperated!"

Hawes roughly yanked up the gag, muffling Lenny once more. "You shot at my sister-in-law and my sister. You attacked my family. Be grateful you're walking out of here alive."

Hawes headed for the door, paying no attention to Lenny's garbled pleas, as if he weren't there at all. Celia followed his lead, leaving another part of her past behind.

Remy spoke briefly to the man standing outside the door, then caught up to where Celia stood waiting with Hawes. "You sure you still want your brother to marry him?" she asked as she draped an arm over Celia's shoulders.

Celia cast Hawes a warm smile, figuring all that chill had to be a heavy burden. "More than ever."

The ice cracked and the man she knew as Chris's fiancé returned to the surface. "Like I said, better." He squeezed Celia's shoulder as he stepped past them, speaking to Holt over the comm. "You got a location?"

Remy's smile was equally genuine, the first Celia had seen on the other woman all night. She was quite attractive when she set the blunt-weapon persona aside. "Helena's a lucky woman."

"So am I."

TWENTY-TWO

"Dimitri not answering your calls?"

Adrian spun from the window he'd been staring out of for the last ten minutes, and the glow of the orange sodium lamp outside reflected in his dark eyes. "What did you do?"

She'd shrug if she could, but the one zip tie binding her arms behind her back and the other binding her to a bolted-down prep table in the vacant catering space Adrian had brought them to didn't allow her much movement. And she didn't want to drop the courthouse pen she had just extracted from her sleeve. "I didn't do anything," she said, keeping Adrian focused on her words and not on the movement behind her back. "But let's talk about what you were trying to do. Win points with Dimitri? And if that didn't work, with Frank?"

"You're a threat to the Bratva. If I removed the queen, then maybe the Madigans wouldn't be coming after us. I thought Dimitri would see that."

Confirmation the Bratva hadn't turned on them and that Frank was effectively an afterthought, not directing this either. "We weren't coming after the Bratva," she said. "Unlike you, we're not stupid. That's why we negotiated with Remy and Dimitri."

"You limited us."

"*Ohhh*," she drawled. "You mean you want the ability to kill indiscriminately with no consequences? Sorry, dude, that's not allowed." She got the cap off the pen, held it in reserve in her one hand, and with the other positioned the pen to press down on the tab of the zip tie holding her to the table, attacking that one first. "We don't care what you do amongst yourselves," she said, continuing to talk and distract while she worked. "But if you harm innocents, we have a problem. Dimitri understands that."

"We didn't have these problems before your brother and you took over."

She smirked. "That's evolution, baby."

At the other end of the prep table, similarly bound, a regrettably awake Dex cursed. "I can't believe Celia is involved with *you*."

"She told you that?"

"Said she was moving on. Well, not with my kids and you. I'm gonna tell the judge and get them back."

Helena rolled her eyes. "Oh please. You have a rap sheet. None of us do. And you're a fucking idiot. I'm guessing you led them to us in the first place."

"I didn't!" He strained against the zip ties, rattling the table and almost making Helena lose the pen. "They came to me, asking all sorts of questions about the shop and you and Celia."

"So you did know who I was at the station Sunday?"

His eyes grew wide. "No!" At least he had the good

sense to be frightened of her, even cuffed. "I didn't know that was *you* they were talking about. Not at first."

He really was fucking dumb, but not her priority right now. She turned her attention back to the man by the window. "Is that right, Adrian? What'd you tell him?"

"Someone's always watching," he said, sparing her a half glance. "Like at that party in November."

Helena froze. Mia and Lily's party. She made a mental note to have Holt check the waitstaff from that night. "Well, they're gonna keep seeing me and Celia together. Her brother's marrying mine, and if I'm lucky, she'll marry me one day too."

"Fuck that," Dex spat. "You can't have her."

She clutched the pen so tight she almost broke it. "She's not a fucking possession, you asshole. Neither are your kids for that matter. She, they, get to make those decisions, not you and not me."

"The both of you shut up!" Zima yelled. He stood in stony stillness, glaring out the window. Waiting. Poor guy thought the cavalry was coming for him. When it didn't after another minute, he got back on the horn again. "I need to talk to Frank," he told someone on the phone.

"Newsflash," Helena said. "He's still not going to take your call."

"Stop egging him on," Dex urged, but she ignored him, keeping her eyes on Zima and her hands busy, detached from the table and working free the second zip tie around her wrists.

Adrian cursed and lowered the phone. Headlights shone through the window and he looked hopeful for a moment, until the car drove past and the lights disappeared.

"Out of options, Adrian?" She continued to loosen the second zip tie. Almost there.

He punched in another number. "Hey, it's Adrian. I need a direct line to Hawes Madigan." Helena detected a woman's voice on the other end, but she couldn't make out the words. Adrian's reddening face told her enough, though. "I'm not telling you what for," Zima said. Ransom, if Helena had to guess. "Just give it to me."

After another few seconds, Zima jammed his finger against the screen and ended the call, cursing again as he shoved the phone back into his pocket.

"Figured it out, did she?" Helena said as she eased her wrists free. She kept them behind her back, not yet letting on that she'd escaped.

"Look, Adrian," Dex said, his tone escalating like the woman's on the phone. "Just let me go. No one wants me. I'm no use to you or anyone."

He turned away from the window, resigned. "Except as a witness." One side of his face was cast in shadow, the other in the sickly glow of the streetlamp. "If I'm going to walk out of here, neither of you can." So he'd decided fleeing was his best option, and killing them was his only option for making that plan work.

Helena couldn't let either of those things happen. Not when she was sure *her* cavalry was minutes away.

He moved closer and drew the gun from his hip holster. The same gun, Helena would bet, that had been used to fire at the shop. He lifted his firing arm toward Dex.

"Really, him first?" Helena scoffed. "Come on, Adrian." She needed him one step closer to her. "I deserve the first shot for all the trouble."

Adrian considered a long moment, then swung the gun her direction. She braced for impact, just in case...

He took a step forward, right where she wanted him.

She planted one foot, stretched, and kicked up the other, knocking the gun out of his hand. Thinking she was still bound, he lunged at her, arms outstretched, hands poised to close around her throat. She intercepted him, relishing the surprised flare of his eyes as she grabbed him by the wrists. The terror in those same eyes as she pushed him up the couple inches she needed. Swinging her legs around his waist, she used her legs and her hands around his wrists to yank him forward and ram his face into the edge of the prep table. Bone crunched, blood splattered onto her, and Adrian screamed in pain. She released his hands and rolled out of the way, narrowly missing being crushed as he fell to the floor.

She wiped a sleeve over her face, clearing it of blood, and quickly scanned the surrounding area, looking for the gun. Her eyes locked on it under the wash table, and her ears locked on the twin roars of a Hog and a Ducati fast approaching outside. She scrabbled across the cement floor for the weapon.

"You bitch." Adrian's hand closed around her ankle.

She stretched for the gun and cursed her lack of inches, the weapon just out of reach. But it wasn't the only weapon available. Twisting over and toward Adrian, she kicked out with her free foot, distracting him so he didn't see the right hook coming. And he sure as fuck didn't see the pen cap she had wedged between her knuckles coming either, the sharp edge connecting directly with his eye.

He roared in pain, and the grip on her ankle disappeared. Freed, she angled on her side and stretched the last few inches for the gun, grabbing it, righting herself, and training the weapon on Adrian as she rose. She had no intention of using it, but Adrian didn't know that. She hadn't fired one in months—they no longer used them—but it was enough to keep Adrian at bay until the overhead lights were flipped on from the breaker box and the building door thrown open. Hawes, garrote in hand, led the group in, with Chris and Avery on his heels, brass knuckles and knives respectively ready, and the rest of her operatives fanning out inside the narrow space.

"Nice of you to join us," Helena said with a victorious smile.

"Looks like you had it handled, kiska." Remy sauntered into the building last, and Adrian's one good eye looked like it was about to blow. He was not happy to see her. Remy crossed to her first, shrugged out of her leather coat, and wrapped it around Helena's shoulders. She stepped back and held out a hand. "I know you don't like these anymore," she said with a nod to the gun. "I can get rid of it for you."

"Generally, true," Helena said, "But I think we might need this one."

She traded Avery the gun for her knife, then approached Dex, who tried and failed to huddle under the table. "Please, don't!"

"I did not go through all this trouble just to kill you." She reached behind him and cut through the zip tie that had bound him to the table, leaving the other ring in place and hauling him up by an arm. "I might want to, but I wouldn't do that to Celia or the kids."

"Oh, thank god, I thought—"

"Don't think," Helena said.

"And listen to me." Hawes stepped directly in front of Dex. "You're gonna tell the cops you shot up the shop."

"You wanted to make sure no one was there so you could break in later," Helena added.

"But—"

"No buts," Helena said. "We're gonna check with Celia, because this is her call, and if she agrees, that's the story."

Dex cut his eyes to Adrian, who sat bleeding on the floor and cowering from Remy. "But he—"

"Isn't gonna walk out of here," Hawes clarified.

The little color left in Dex's face bled the rest of the way out.

"But you are," Helena said, offering him a shiny nickel of reassurance. "Unless you want to stay with him."

Dex finally—*finally*—shut his fucking mouth.

"That's what I thought."

She handed Dex to Chris, who told her, "Someone outside wants to see you."

By his sly smile, she had no doubt who was out there waiting for her. Her first instinct was to question it—Why was Celia there?—but she caught herself. Reflected on what she'd just told Dex, what she herself had decided in the courtroom. All the evidence pointed to Celia being the strongest woman she knew. She loved and protected her own as fiercely as Helena and her brothers did. So of course she was there. Helena wouldn't question that decision.

She zipped up the coat Remy had loaned her, covering the bloody mess on her sweater, and strode out the door. The previously deserted parking lot was full of cars, but Helena had no trouble spotting Celia. She stood next to Victoria by the Benz in a halo of light from a streetlamp, fucking gorgeous as always. Helena crossed the space as fast as her legs would carry her, just shy of a run.

"Hey, baby, I'm sor—"

Celia didn't let her finish, clasping both sides of her face and drawing her in for a deep claiming kiss. Helena sighed, adrenaline receding, happy to let Celia be the strong one for a few blissful seconds.

Closer to thirty later, Celia gentled the kiss, her thumbs wiping what could only be more blood off her cheeks, not the least bit fazed. "You're okay?" Celia asked.

Helena nodded. "It's not mine. I'm okay." She lightly held Celia's wrists and lowered her hands, wrapping them in hers between them. "Are you okay with us? With there being an us?"

"More than. If you are."

Helena shifted her slightly and drew her into another kiss. Celia smiled against her lips. "You moved me so Dex would see, didn't you?"

"I did," Helena admitted with a wink, then sobered, having to address the fucking idiot in the room. Or rather in the parking lot. "We need to talk about what to do with him."

Celia shifted them a second time, even more directly into Dex's line of sight. "After I kiss you again."

Fuck, she was perfect. And perfect for her. "I think you might be the dangerous one in this relationship."

And she proved it, laying a kiss on Helena that was full of desire and confidence and just the right amount of danger for both their hearts.

TWENTY-THREE

Helena made a loop of the house to confirm everyone's location and level of distraction—Holt sleeping in his room for a spell; Gloria and Mia entertaining Lily in the next room over; Hawes, Chris, and Marco playing a video game in the living room—then followed the smell of Italian sausage and Daisy's and Tulip's *meows* to the kitchen. Helena double tapped the door frame as she entered, making her presence known.

Celia smiled over her shoulder. "You don't have to do that. I'm getting used to turning around and you being there."

"It's not too much, is it?" Helena said.

Except for the time she'd had to spend in court and Celia in the shop that afternoon, Helena hadn't strayed far from Celia's side the past twenty-four hours—not at the station last night, not as they'd dozed off together first against the wall in Mia's room, then against the wall in Marco's, and not as they'd otherwise moved about the house all day.

"Not at all," Celia said as she covered a casserole dish with plastic wrap. "Wouldn't mind if you were closer."

Helena liked the sound of that invitation. Snuggling close behind Celia, she wrapped her arms around her waist and poked her head around Celia's shoulder. "Whatcha making?"

"Sausage strata for breakfast tomorrow. It's the kids' favorite, and I figure after I kept disrupting their routine this week…"

"You're letting them play hooky tomorrow for the wedding rehearsal." They were two weeks out from Hawes and Chris's big day, but the rehearsal had to be scheduled ahead of time, given the Maritime Museum's schedule. "I don't think they're gonna object."

"It's also my favorite."

"Now the truth comes out." She snuck her hands beneath the hem of Celia's tee and spread her fingers over her abdomen, enjoying the heat that rushed to meet her hands. "You know…" She nuzzled behind Celia's ear, inhaling the Dove soap and lingering smell of shop grease she hoped Celia never lost. "Hawes can cook too. Just give him a recipe."

Celia dipped her chin and smiled, an attractive blush pinking her cheeks. Helena was officially smitten. "What's that smile about?" she asked as she untangled from around Celia and claimed a stool at the island.

Celia picked up the dish and carried it to the fridge, the cats chasing the scent and the frayed ends of Celia's pajama bottoms. "Yesterday, I told Hawes, after we got you back, I just wanted to be the partner who was the mom-friend and who made sure you all were fed and taken care of."

Partner. Helena's heart skipped at the prospect, never having thought it in the cards for her. Never having thought it would be someone outside their world. But Oak had been right. Celia was just what she needed, what they all needed. And if Helena wanted a chance at a future with Celia, they needed to talk about the past week. "Even after yesterday?" She waited for Celia to close the fridge, then waved her over to stand between her knees. "You know more of what you're getting into now. Are you sure you still want to be here?"

"This is already my family. We lost Chris for ten years. Not letting that happen again."

Hands on her waist, Helena tugged her closer even as she offered her a final out. "But you don't have to be *this* close."

Celia closed the rest of the distance between them and draped her arms over Helena's shoulders. "I don't have to be, but I want to be. But, Helena, no more pushing me away. My mental health can't handle that, not after Dex, and frankly, I shouldn't have to, not if this is going to be a real partnership."

"I want that too, and I'm willing to work for it, including therapy if we need it. Hell, I probably need it." She flitted a hand in the general direction of her head. "There's a lot up here I've ignored for too long." Her parents' death, her grandmother's and Amelia's betrayals, the mounting stress of her everyday juggling act. Oak had a point the other day, though Helena suspected some of her stress might ease with Celia to come home to at night.

Celia softly kissed her forehead. "I'll get you the name of someone."

"Thank you, and I am sorry for icing you out, Cee." She

glanced up through her lashes. "I tried to apologize yesterday, but someone hauled off and kissed me."

"I'm not sorry about that," Celia said with a shrug.

"Figured not, but I am about the way I treated you. I was just trying to protect you, but I realize that's your call. I'm sorry for not letting you make it."

"The safest place for me and my family is right here with you and yours. You and your brothers have made sure of that in a dozen different ways. Don't throw all that work away. And trust that you've made me strong enough to protect myself too."

Helena clasped her hands behind Celia's waist, holding tight. "Might take a little practice."

Celia chuckled and pecked her lips. "Expected it might. I want to keep practicing too."

"Count on it." Helena drew her in for a longer, lingering kiss. "More practicing this too. You all done in here?"

Celia smiled against her lips. "Yep."

Helena slid off the stool, flush against Celia's body, exactly where she'd wanted to be the past twenty-four hours. Longer than that. And she was done waiting, the building ache between her legs demanding relief. "Let's go *practice*."

They wandered out of the kitchen, hand in hand, but when Celia moved to go upstairs, Helena directed her the opposite direction. "Somewhere else I've been fantasizing about."

An even brighter blush streaked across Celia's cheeks. "But there's no door. Anyone could—"

Helena smirked. "There are still some tricks to this house you Perris don't know yet." She shooed the cats toward the living room to harass the guys and led Celia down the stairs to the home gym. They rounded the corner, and Celia gasped.

"Helena, what—

"My fantasy and your fantasy." And totally worth the effort of squirreling away sheets and votive candles, and keeping everyone out of the gym today, so she could see the soft candlelight reflected off Celia's enchanted and surprised face. She jostled Celia loose from her shock, moved her fully inside the room, and flipped up the light panel, revealing the keypad underneath. She entered the test code—not wanting the rest of the house to lockdown—and the crenellations on either side of the open doorway folded back. A steel pocket door slid out, completely blocking the entrance.

Celia stumbled back. "What the hell?"

"Panic room."

Celia surveyed the space anew, as if looking past the two dozen candles and cotton-sheet covered mats. A smile spread across her face, realization dawning. "A panic room with all your weapons."

"Precisely." Helena closed the panel and guided Celia onto the mats. "We're also at least a floor below our family, in what amounts to an insulated bunker." She grabbed the hem of her own shirt and removed it, tossing it into the corner. Celia's hot stare raked across her chest, and Helena hoped she liked how the spreading blush looked against the lavender shelf bra she'd put on for the occasion. She moved into Celia's space, wanting her to feel the radiating heat and desire, wanting her to know how much she was wanted. Helena swept her hands under the back of Celia's shirt and kissed a path up her neck to her ear. "I want to hear you scream."

Celia shivered in her arms but recovered quickly, dipping her hands inside the back of Helena's pants and over her satin underwear, the cool fabric and light friction delicious against Helena's skin. "Thank you for this," Celia said. "In case I'm too hoarse from screaming to tell you later."

"Fuck, Cee, now you've gone and done it." She nipped Celia's ear then drew back, stripping the shirt off over Celia's head and revealing a sexy red lace number. Her dark hair fell around her shoulders, tousled and wild, stealing Helena's breath. She was so fucking beautiful, body and soul, and Helena was so fucking lucky to get a shot with her. She lowered onto her knees, ready to worship, and as she pulled Celia's pajama bottoms down, exposing a matching red lace thong, Helena's mouth watered. She hooked her thumbs in either side of Celia's barely there underwear. "You always wear such sexy things under your clothes."

"Just 'cause there's grease under my fingernails doesn't mean I don't also like pretty things." She trailed a finger over the lacy edge of one of her bra cups. "Dex thought lingerie was a waste of money, but it was something for me."

Helena leaned forward, nuzzling the baby soft skin below Celia's belly button. "You're next birthday…" She nipped along the top lacy edge of the thong. "We'll fly to London and Paris. Buy you a whole fucking trunkful."

"I'd like that," Celia said, breathy and rough, and Helena couldn't resist dragging her thumbs down the outer edges of the thong, swiping them under the narrowing fabric, finding Celia wet for her. A hand tangled in Helena's hair. "Would also like to see the rest of what you put on for me."

She swiped her thumbs over Celia's damp lips once more, barely resisting the urge to pull them apart and torture Celia's clit with her tongue through the lace. That would come, so would Celia, but first, she'd do whatever Celia asked. She stood, peeled her pants off, and righted herself to find Celia's gaze positively ravenous. "Are they all pastels?" she asked as she trailed her fingers over the swells of Helena's tits.

"I needed to keep something light close to me," she confessed. She had to be smarter and deadlier than everyone, but this part of her could be soft without giving away any weakness. Except to Celia. "But now I have you."

"You are a remarkable woman, Helena Madigan." She cupped one of her tits, and Helena leaned more of her weight into Celia. *Swooned*, she thought, was the technical term. First time for everything. "All of you."

"So are you." She nipped the end of Celia's chin. "Now fucking kiss me."

Celia didn't need to be told twice, and once her tongue plunged inside Helena's mouth, Helena was lost. And lost had never felt so fucking good. Tangled up with Celia, in her touch and taste, in her body as Helena urged her down to the mat, laid her out, and fucking feasted. First on her breasts, pulling them out of their cups and working the nipples into tight aching peaks. Then kissing down her torso, swirling a tongue inside her belly button, before burying her face between Celia's thighs in the patch of dark coarse hair there. She tortured herself and Celia, licking, kissing, and nipping through and around the lace thong, sneaking her tongue under the fabric every so often to get a direct hit because she couldn't get enough of the keening sound Celia made each time she did it, of the quiver of her thighs under her hands, of the way she rocked harder against her mouth, of the rich musky fragrance that continued to intensify.

"You need something, Cee?" she asked.

"More." Celia palmed her tits, pinching her nipples, as if that could somehow release the pressure Helena had been building, for both of them. "Inside, please."

"I do this..." Helena hooked her thumbs inside the straps of the thong. "I wanna hear you scream. You got that, Cee?"

She nodded frantically, close but needing a bit more, and Helena was ready to give it to her. She yanked the thong down, then trailed her hands back up the inside of Celia's thighs on a direct path to her cunt. She trailed two fingers through the wet folds and around Celia's clit, circling. She moved to bend over, to taste and touch with nothing between her tongue and Celia's slick, hot skin, but Celia bent a leg, blocking her.

"Wait." Panting, she levered up on one elbow, lust dazed but determined. "You too."

Helena had been largely ignoring the throb between her own thighs, of the wetness soaking the crotch of her own underwear, but Celia offering to bring her along for the ride shattered her focus. Brought to mind all the positions and scenarios that would work to get them off together. "Sixty-nine?" she said.

Apprehension tiptoed across Celia's face, and Helena laid a reassuring hand on her stomach. It had taken her a while to work up to oral sex too, with men and women. "We'll get there. I've got another idea."

She moved to take off her bra and underwear, but Celia stopped her again. "Leave it on. It's sexy."

Helena arched a brow. "Payback for the shop?"

"You bet."

Laughing, a first for Helena during sex, she leaned over and gave Celia a deep plundering kiss and was surprised when Celia groaned hungrily, apparently liking the taste of herself. Maybe she'd get there quicker than Helena had. For now, though, her plan was set. She tore her lips away and moved to Celia's side, on hands and knees, mouth and hand where she could reach Celia's cunt, legs spread so Celia could reach hers. She took Celia's hand in hers and directed it between her legs.

Celia caught on fast, slipping her fingers inside Helena's underwear and over her folds. Helena sighed, bowing up when Celia's fingers circled her clit. "That's it, baby." She spent a good minute or two riding Celia's hand, letting Cee build her up, get into a rhythm, before she put her mouth back on Celia and a finger inside her.

"Oh fuck!" Celia shouted and pounded the mat with her free hand. Her other hand moved faster on Helena's clit. "Oh fuck, please!" She demanded with her fingers too, dipping inside Helena, and Helena lost her rhythm for a moment, too caught up in riding the waves of building pleasure, until Celia returned to circling her nub, increasingly frantic.

"I'm close, Helena. I'm close!"

Helena briefly lifted her face, reminding Celia of her duty. "I wanna hear it, Cee."

She nodded, her fingers moving faster against the bundle of nerves driving Helena wild, and Helena, building at a rapid clip too, used two fingers to fill Celia, pumping, her tongue on her clit, flicking, and Celia tipped the rest of the way over the edge with a full-throated "Fuck me!" Her cunt greedily clenched around Helena's fingers, the tight heat causing Helena to buck against Celia's hand, the extra pressure all she needed to come too. She grabbed Celia's wrist, shoved her hand back, and following the cue, Celia sank her fingers inside Helena, filling her up as her walls rippled with pleasure.

Once the waves had subsided, Celia withdrew her fingers, as did Helena. She sank onto the mat, on her side, her head resting on Celia's abdomen, an arm thrown over her middle, both of them catching their breaths in contented silence and company.

Celia's fingertips coasted up and down her forearm, gentle and soothing. "Did I scream loud enough for you?"

"I don't know. You've still got your voice."

"I guess you'll have to try harder next time."

Helena swatted her belly. "Oh, I can go harder, baby."

"I want to try all the things with you." She threaded her fingers through her hair, pushing back a wild hank that was tickling Helena's eyelashes. "Maybe even loving you…"

And didn't that just tickle her heart too. Helena dropped a kiss on her hip, a future in front of her that she'd never expected. One full of family and love, trips to London and Paris for lingerie, and nights in the arms of this amazing woman. "I'd like to give that a try too."

TWENTY-FOUR

Celia strolled through the Maritime Museum's exhibits, waiting for the rest of the wedding party to gather as the guests outside began to take their seats. It was a gorgeous setup for the wedding, ribboned white chairs and an abundance of flowers on the brick patio overlooking the Bay. Not as gorgeous, however, as the blond who stepped between her and the windows.

"Well, hello there, Miss Perri," Helena said with a smirk.

Celia returned it. "Hello there, Miss Madigan." She snagged the open lapels of the borrowed judge's robe Helena had donned for the occasion and tugged her girl-friend closer. The black robe was a sharp, striking contrast to the ice blue dress Helena wore beneath it. The same color as Celia's dress but a different cut, each of them picking a style that suited them best. "Don't you look all official today?"

Helena leaned in for a kiss, which Celia returned, though not as fervently as she would have liked, careful not to mess up their makeup. Helena drew back and zipped up the robe. "Closest I'll ever get to these."

"You regret that?"

"Heck no." She handed Celia her folio and adjusted the robe on her shoulders. "One, this thing is hot and scratchy. Two, I can do more good on this side of the bench."

Celia gave her a deeper kiss, damn the makeup. "You're remarkable."

Helena smiled against her lips. "So are you." When they came up for air, Celia thumbed away an errant smudge of lipstick she'd left on Helena, who did the same for her. "You know what else is remarkable?" Helena said. "This weather. How did they get this lucky?"

Despite the rainiest January in Celia's recent memory, her brother had managed to get perfect weather on his wedding day—a balmy seventy degrees and not a rain cloud or fog bank in sight. "They deserve it."

"Can't argue that."

But someone was arguing, Lily's whimpers a sound-track to the rough and weary voices behind a nearby exhibit wall. "I'm surprised you showed up," Holt said.

"Do you want me to leave?" Brax replied.

Celia shot a worried glance at Helena, who lifted a hand, signaling to wait.

"Of course I don't want you to leave," Holt said. "You're family. This is supposed to be a happy day for *our* family."

Lily's whimpers escalated to soft cries as if sensing her Da-Da and Ba-Ba arguing.

"I'll go," Brax said.

"Cap, don't, please."

"Ba-Ba!" Lily chipped in, and Celia knew Brax's heart had to be breaking.

Holt's too. "Why are you pushing us away?"

"I don't know if I can do this anymore."

Celia rubbed a hand over her chest, her heart aching for how much that must have hurt Brax to say and for how much it must have hurt Holt to hear.

"Is this about what Chris said last summer?"

As Gloria approached with Mia and Marco, Celia shot Helena another look. They couldn't wait any longer. "I got it," Helena said, heading the direction of Holt's and Brax's voices.

"Are you guys looking forward to the trolley?" Celia asked, aiming to distract her kids from the nearby argument.

Marco fiddled with his light blue bowtie. "Think they'll let me drive it?"

Mia, in a matching blue dress, slapped his hand away. "Leave it alone, and no you can't drive it. You don't have a license."

"It's on tracks," Marco countered. "I can push a handle."

"I'm more interested in the food after," Gloria said. "Never thought I'd be going to a wedding reception at Gary Danko."

Neither had Celia. Before Chris had met Hawes for the first time at Danko, Celia had never visited the famous San Francisco establishment. Now, it was a regular go-to for Madigan-Perri family events, including today's wedding. She half suspected Chris and Hawes had picked the Maritime Museum for their nuptials because it was a short walk—or trolley ride—to the restaurant.

"Ooh, yeah," Marco said. "Especially the dessert table."

"You better not eat everything on it before we get there,"

Chris said, entering arm in arm with his very-soon-to-be husband.

Gloria shook a finger at them both. "You're not supposed to see each other yet."

"Oh, I just saw him," Chris said with a cheeky grin. "In the coat closet."

The kids snickered, and Celia bit her lip to keep from doing the same. Helena saved her the near chastisement, appearing from around the exhibit, her stride determined. "We ready to rock and roll?" she said.

Hawes lifted Chris's hand, kissing his knuckles. "Never been more ready."

"Little H?" Helena called.

Holt joined them, eyes red rimmed, but with a smile plastered on his face for his brother. "I'm here."

As Helena spoke to Avery at the exit door and Gloria got everyone in line, Celia laid a hand on Holt's forearm. "You okay?"

"Not exactly."

Celia followed his gaze out the window, to Brax, Lily in his arms, as he walked up the side aisle and took his seat in the front row. The love and fear in Holt's warm brown eyes were heartbreaking. She rose on her toes and kissed his cheek. "Give Brax a chance," she said, parroting back the advice Holt had given her and remembering the conversation she'd had that day with Brax at the station. "He'll come around. I promise."

Holt released a shaky breath, took a deeper one, then smiled, a small but real one. "Thanks, Cee."

Outside, the music started, and the crowd shifted in their seats, angling to see the coming processional. Helena, on her way to the back of the line with Hawes, stopped at

Celia's side and stole another kiss. "Whatever you said to Holt, thank you."

"Whatever is wrong," Celia replied, "we'll get through it as a family."

Helena's mission-critical face softened, transforming into the soft, peaceful one Celia had made it her own mission to bring about at least once a day, more if she could manage it. Doing whatever she could to take care of Helena too. "You know I love you, right?"

Celia did, even if the surprise of Helena saying it for the first time blinded her for a second. But she recovered quickly, smiling wide. "Good, because I love you too."

"Hello, this is *our* wedding," Chris teased from behind them.

"Yeah, yeah, Mr. Hair, we know."

Everyone laughed, and they parted reluctantly, Celia taking her position on Chris's arm, Helena on Hawes's. Just in time as the glass doors opened, and Holt and Gloria were first down the aisle. The kids followed, and then it was her and Chris's turn.

At the end of the aisle, they stopped, and Celia rose on her toes, kissing her brother's cheek. "I know I've said this before, but I'm proud of you. And thank you for giving us more family."

Chris hugged her tight and dropped a kiss on the crown of her head. "I'm proud of you too, Cee, and I think we've got you to thank for the family part too."

They shared a smile, then took their places at the front, waiting for Hawes and Helena. Looking out over their gathered friends and family, at Hawes walking down the aisle, no lingering chill about him as he smiled adoringly at Chris, at the similar smile aimed Celia's direction from the woman on Hawes's arm, Celia couldn't hold back her own smile. Couldn't hold in the happiness that surrounded and buoyed her. Her family was stronger than ever, and she was happy to have played a part in making that—making this special day—happen. And she couldn't wait to see how their family—how she and Helena—continued to grow in the future.

Don't stop now!
Read Holt & Kane's story, *Silent Knight*!

Want more sapphic romance?
My steamy sapphic romance, *Over a Barrel*, is out now!

For all the latest updates on new projects, sneak peeks, and more, sign up for Layla's Newsletter.

Reviews are an invaluable tool when it comes to spreading the word about great reads. Please consider leaving an honest review for *Queen's Ransom* on your favorite review site.

Thank you for reading!

ACKNOWLEDGMENTS

It only took a year-and-a-half (a longer-than-long-please-let's-never-ever-do-that-again year-and-a-half) but *Fog City* is finally back, and I'm thrilled to share Helena and Celia's story with you. This one is a first for me, and I hope the first of many more to come.

I wouldn't have been able to do this without your continued excitement and support of me and these characters. Special thanks to my readers in the Lushes Facebook Group who cheer every time I post a snippet, to Kim who helps author-me function, and to my sprint groups and author pals, especially Erin McLellan, Allison Temple, Annabeth Albert, Riley Hart, Anna Zabo, and Hailey Turner, whose dedication is an inspiration that keeps my own words flowing.

Thank you to the team that makes *Fog City* look and read amazing: Wander Aguiar and models Amanda and Tiffany for the gorgeous cover photography, Cate Ashwood for the amazing cover design, Kim and Rachel for the beta reads and snippet input, Kristi Yanta for the series plot doctoring, Susie Selva for the pep talks, homemade jam, Dunkin' gift cards, and top-shelf editing, and Lori Parks for the quick-turn proofreading eyes.

Finally, thanks to Nina, Kelley, Kim, Kayti and the entire Valentine PR Team and to Leslie and the GRR Team for your support and coordinated efforts in spreading the word about this book and *Fog City*!

ALSO BY LAYLA REYNE

For the most up-to-date list of titles and a helpful reading order, please visit www.laylareyne.com.

Agents Irish and Whiskey:

Single Malt

Cask Strength

Barrel Proof

Tequila Sunrise

Blended Whiskey

Angel's Share

Trouble Brewing:

Imperial Stout

Craft Brew

Noble Hops

Final Gravity

Fog City:

Prince of Killers

King Slayer

A New Empire

Queen's Ransom

Silent Knight

Perfect Play:

Dead Draw

Bad Bishop

King Hunt

Best Play

Redemption Inc.:

The Accidental

The Bounty

The Martyr

The Boss

More Romantic Suspense / Mystery:

What We May Be

Variable Onset

Soul to Find:

Icarus and the Devil

Jason and the Storm

Paris and the Reaper

Atlas and the Traitor

Table for Two:

The Last Drop

Dine With Me

Blue Plate Special

Over a Barrel

The Sweet Spot

Sigh of Relief

Changing Lanes:

Relay

Medley

Freestyle

More Contemporary Romance:

Barn Burner

Eyes on You

ABOUT THE AUTHOR

Layla Reyne is the author of *What We May Be* and the *Agents Irish and Whiskey*, *Fog City*, and *Perfect Play* series. She writes sexy, intense LGBTQIA+ romance featuring competent adults in kitchens, sports arenas, car chases, and other high-stakes situations. Whether it's adrenaline-fueled suspense, rival athletes, vampires and shifters, or love mixed with mouth-watering foodie goodness, queer folks finding happily-ever-afters is guaranteed.

You can find Layla online at laylareyne.com and at the following sites:

BB bookbub.com/authors/layla-reyne

f facebook.com/laylareyne

⊙ instagram.com/laylareyne

♪ tiktok.com/@laylareyne

🦋 bsky.app/profile/laylareyne